BEFORE

—

Carmen Boullosa

TRANSLATED FROM THE SPANISH BY
PETER BUSH

INTRODUCTION BY
PHILLIP LOPATE

DEEP VELLUM PUBLISHING

DALLAS, TEXAS

Deep Vellum Publishing
3000 Commerce St., Dallas, Texas 75226
deepvellum.org · @deepvellum

Deep Vellum Publishing is a 501c3
nonprofit literary arts organization founded in 2013.

ISBN: 978-1-941920-28-2 (paperback) · 978-1-941920-29-9 (ebook)
LIBRARY OF CONGRESS CONTROL NUMBER: 2015960721
—
Cover design & typesetting by Anna Zylicz · annazylicz.com

Text set in Bembo, a typeface modeled on typefaces cut by Francesco Griffo
for Aldo Manuzio's printing of *De Aetna* in 1495 in Venice.

Distributed by Consortium Book Sales & Distribution.

Printed in the United States of America on acid-free paper.

Praise for Texas: The Great Theft

Nominated for the INTERNATIONAL DUBLIN LITERARY AWARD 2016
Shortlisted for the PEN TRANSLATION AWARD 2015
Winner of the TYPOGRAPHICAL ERA TRANSLATION AWARD 2015
World Literature Today's 75 NOTABLE TRANSLATIONS of 2014

"Brutal, poetic, hilarious and humane…a masterly crafted tale."
—SJÓN, author of *From the Mouth of the Whale*

"Utterly entertaining—a comic tour de force. I loved the book and think it deserves a very wide readership."
—PHILIP LOPATE author of *Portrait Inside My Head*

"Boullosa's tale evokes a history that couldn't be more relevant to today's immigration battles in the US."
—JANE CIABATTARI, BBC

"Boullosa's tour de force account of this bloody legacy…is not a documentary. Rather, it is satire at its highest, presenting numerous grotesque biographies of the alien invaders, while also lightly reviewing the genres that have made Wild West literature part of the national identity and psyche."
—NICOLÁS KANELLOS, *Review: Literature and Arts of the Americas*

"Many of the events in Texas seem as if they just happened yesterday… It's a story that shows the foundation of many border issues today."
—MERCEDES OLIVERA, *Dallas Morning News*

"Boullosa is one of Mexico's most respected writers and, with a book as rich as this under her belt, it's not difficult to understand why…We're introduced to a cast list so extensive it rivals Dickens and a novel of such depth and scope that I can't resist comparing it to Tolstoy's work."
— GARY PERRY, Foyle's Bookstore (LONDON, UK)

"Historical fiction at its very best, avoiding all semblance of caricature or appeals to stereotype. The classic Western."
— *San Francisco Chronicle*

"What is both moving and also lucid about Boullosa's prose, though, is her ability to take one in and out of a scene fraught with disorder and violence, and place one back in the rich spirit of humility encountering sublime beauty."
—MATT PINCUS, *Bookslut*

"Think *Catch-22* on the Mexican border. A surprisingly funny, intensely complex and occasionally shocking take on the revisionist Western."
—JUSTIN SOUTHER, Malaprops Bookstore (ASHEVILLE, NC)

"Evidence that our ideas about postmodern cowpoke tales have been woefully premature…What is outstanding in Boullosa's work is the deep sympathy expressed for every human encountered."
— ROBERTO ONTIVEROS, *Dallas Morning News*

To José María Espinasa,
to Jonás Aguirre Liguori, when you were still unborn
to María José Boullosa, who I hope is resting peacefully

Those of you who felt the heart beat of night
those who through relentless insomnia heard
the shutting of a door, the echo of a distant car
a vague shuddering, a slight noise…

In the moments of mysterious silence,
when the forgotten arise from their prisons,
at the hour of the dead, at the hour of repose,
you can read these lines drenched in bitterness…

As into a glass I pour them from my sorrow
distant memories and sombre misfortunes
the sad nostalgias of my flower-drunk soul,
the mourning of my party-sorrowed heart,

The pain of not being what I should have been,
the loss of the realm that was made for me,
the thought that at one moment I might not have been,
the dream my life has known since I was born…

All this comes amid the deep silence
which night wraps around earthly illusion,
and I feel an echo as from the heart of the world
which penetrates and moves my own.

Rubén Darío

INTRODUCTION
Phillip Lopate

Before, like Scheherezade, she produced her thousand and one novels, short stories, poems, plays, pamphlets, essay collections and literary critiques, before she wrote her historical fictions about Cleopatra, Caribbean pirates, Cervantes on the battlefield on Lepanto, and nineteenth century Texas border skirmishes, before she did her investigative reports of contemporary narco-terrorism and her rediscoveries of neglected women writers, Carmen Boullosa wrote *Before* (*Antes*), a haunting and haunted novella. It was brought out in 1989 by Vuelta, the publishing house founded and run by Octavio Paz. She was thirty-five years old at the time, and received the prestigious Xavier Villaurrutia Prize for this novella, and for a volume of her poems and an essay collection also published that year. You might say, however, that *Before* launched her, and she has been soaring ever since.

We turn to it now with the realization that there can already be found here many quintessential Boullosa stylistics and preoccupations: the rush of urgent speech, teetering between humor and panic; the agreeable pact with melancholy; the appearance of grotesque, supernatural and sensually erotic elements in everyday life; the female body as a contested site of wayward power and unrest.

On a superficial level, the book is a compendium of childhood memories, touching almost randomly on ecstasy, shame, confusion, pleasure, envy, pride—the sort of material one expects to find in an autobiographical novel by an emerging writer. But several elements render it decidedly odd. First, it purports to be told by a ghost: the narrator states that she is dead, and therefore is summoning memories from the grave—though there is very little ghostlike about her, other than this assertion. There is none of the usual attention paid in ghost stories to the mechanics of mobility or corporeality, and the narrative voice is so lively, so present, that some readers may be tempted to refuse to believe that the protagonist is in fact dead, and treat the claim solely as a metaphor (perhaps to the author's horror), while still fully enjoying the tale. Second, the narrator keeps insisting that Esther, who is clearly her mother, is not her mother. Since she seems genuinely fond of the woman, this refusal appears, on the face of it, perverse if not inexplicable. Toward the end of the book, Esther even cries out, "Please say mom at least now!" and the girl finally relents, crying, "Oh Esther, I loved you so much, so much, Mom, Mom, Mom, Mom…" At which point the mother dies.

Why these two conceits? They might initially be seen as a deriving from an experimental mindset. Boullosa's first novel, *Better Disappeared*, was an even more experimental text, and it set up the trope of Woman as in danger of being erased or negated, which is carried further along in *Before*. Perhaps the author, a feminist, was trying to say something about the difficulty of women asserting a self in Mexico's patriarchal macho society. But I think there is more to it than that. Allow me to fall into the vulgar error of bringing certain personal facts about the author's life into an analysis of a work of fiction.

Boullosa's mother, a psychologist, died when she was 15. Not long after, her father remarried, and Carmen did not get along with her stepmother. This was a very traumatic period for her: losing her mother cleaved her childhood in two, between a "before" and "after," you might say. It seems to me the mother's death is central to this novella. The book begins by stressing the narrator's fear: "my fear, my panic, my terror." Children are often afraid, but later on in the text the narrator tells us she was not the kind of kid to be afraid of the dark, or be thrown by little disturbances: she was in fact "brave." So this particular fear could be a presentiment, the terror of possibly losing her mother, the worst thing that could happen to a child. Turning herself into a ghost (playing dead) and refusing to acknowledge that her mother is her mother would be two ways to avoid the full impact of that grief.

The unnamed protagonist's fear is characterized as a response to certain "noises" or, more often, "steps" that keep pursuing her, like in *Cat People*, that classy horror movie by Val Lewton, It could be argued that she is afraid not only of her mother dying, but of her body's impending physiological changes. For those raised in a sexually repressive all-girls' Catholic school, puberty can seem both catastrophic and liberating, and the blood of menstruation loom as simultaneously Gothic and normal. When the protagonist's period finally comes, it coincides with the mother's death, as though there were a causal link; and the narrator even expresses guilt by saying "it was my fault." By becoming a woman, she has both emulated and competed with her mother, thereby "annihilating" her—just as, earlier, she had encroached on her artist mother's field by doing some peculiar drawings.

Boullosa intentionally invites us to conflate her heroine with herself by having the narrator state matter-of-factly that she was born in 1954 in Mexico City, exactly as was the author. She also makes a point of insisting that "everything I've told you is real. I haven't invented a single word, I've written my descriptions trying as much as possible to stick to the facts." But here I think she is playing with us, fudging the meta-line between nonfiction and fiction. For starters, Boullosa gives the narrator two older, distant, chilly half-sisters, while she herself had a home packed with half a dozen younger siblings. No doubt there are many other deviations from life in the book.

More important than invention is the estranging, ritualizing angle of vision Boullosa applies to seemingly ordinary objects and mundane occurrences. Scissors pursue, eucalyptus trees sabotage, an embroidery needle pierces the maid's hand, a turtle bleeds, red nail polish on a nipple becomes stigmata, panties get swiped while sitting on the toilet, petticoats turn up burned. "Making it strange" is of course a recognized part of the modernist aesthetic. It is also very Latin American. Though magic realism has become a tired, somewhat debased concept, one can nevertheless detect in Boullosa's work certain correspondences with, say, Juan Rulfo's intermingling of the living and the dead, or her friend Roberto Bolaño's maximalist loquacity, or Borges' rationalist love of fantasy, or Adolfo Bioy-Casares' mastery of the novella form, or Clarise Lispector's weird, body-obsessed stories. Boullosa's magic is certainly more cheerful than Lispector's: it begins as a child's sense of wonder, then suffers loss of innocence, only to surface again as worldly re-enchantment. The heroine is no angel, and she gladly indulges in bad behavior from time to time as proof of her obstinate agency. Still, she is stunned to find that she can betray a friend so easily, or deface an expensive article of clothing for no reason. That the world is still a mystifying place, touched by the sometimes bitter, sometimes amusingly picaresque recognition of everyone's robust capacity to act self-servingly, goes a long way toward accounting for that comic spirit which is irrepressibly present in all of Carmen Boullosa's writing.

We may also note her tonal humor, seen in the proliferation of exclamation points and rhetorical questions, the alternation of brusque statements with long chattering sentences, like the schoolgirls playing the game of "conversation," imitating old ladies. Boullosa's vigorously conversational style maintains a steady, intimate bond with her readers, even as it keeps us off-balance. Less noticeable, perhaps, is a current of anger that runs underneath the humor and high spirits, as when our protagonist thrashes a girl who had snatched her sister's valise: "they tried to pull me off her, but the rage I felt was such that it wouldn't let me open my jaws as the leg owner shrieked..." In Boullosa, there is always a trace of political anger or protest. Among other things, *Before* is a subtle portrait of the Mexican upper-middle class, circa late '50s-early '60s, who expect nothing but service from the lower classes. They seem shielded from the heavier blows of life, which is why the mother's death comes as such a shock, almost an obscenity. This novella, germinated in grief, or what Thomas Mann called "disorder and early sorrow," has been transformed through Boullosa's literary art and salutary detachment into a lyrical, playful gem.

New York City, February 2016

I

Where were we before we got to this point? Didn't they tell you? Who could tell you if you had nobody to ask? And do you yourself remember? How could you remember? Particularly as you're not here…And if I keep on? Well, if I keep on perhaps you'll show up.

How would I like you to be? I'd like you to be whatever you were! Just warm, not necessarily hot, a piece of dough, to touch, to feel…I'd be happy to feel something, feel it gently, to caress without scratching or hurting and with nothing but nothing at all left on my hands…nothing at all…not a single mark…

But nobody's with me. Nobody, apart from my fear, my panic, my terror…Fear of whom? There's no way I can be afraid! I've shown in a thousand ways how harmless I am, like a duck on the lakeside waiting for children to throw me a scrap of food or leave something in the paper they carelessly drop…But they're disgusted by me, disgusted, disgusted is the word. I dirtied their "day out in the country," dirtied their lakeside breakfast, turned their breakfast haven into a sludgy mess…kids, I'm like you, leave something for me, someone wait for me, stay with me, just for a second, come on, kids!

They leave. Their Dad will take them straight to school now. They didn't have that disappointed look of wanting to breakfast here…

But I'll start at the beginning. Sure, I was like those children, I was one of those awkward children, and here I am cut off from their world forever. Children! I was like you once!

I really must overcome my fear and start telling my story.

I was born in Mexico City in 1954. I clearly remember the day I was born. The fear, naturally, I understand her and don't reproach her—perhaps if I got to be in her situation (I never imagine I could be so lucky) I'd also feel afraid.

The fear was because of grandmother, not to do with me. What about me? I still couldn't see myself…I was so defenseless…More defenseless than any child of my age, than any other newly born child.

I return to the fear, a woman's fear: the young woman bathed in sweat, her body suffering the violence of birth stripped of all coquettish charms, visibly beautiful. That day she was paler than usual and when I saw her for the first time every small feature reflected the fear I never imagined would spring upon me and lock its jaw.

Her name was completely different to mine. More resonant, a name I'd give to a son if I had one. Her name was Esther.

Although I'd always seen her in a very distinctive light, I loved her as much as if she were my mother.

How long did it take me to realize she wasn't my mother? I always knew, but up to the day they came for me, everything acted as if she were.

On the other hand I don't remember him that night. What was he doing? I'll say he was at work, give him the benefit of the doubt, but when I saw her pallor, the strange mess between her sheets and the cold (pitiless and uncaring) hands around her, I understood everything. What good was her defiant beauty if the man she wanted wouldn't love her? Perhaps she was too beautiful to be loved by anyone. I don't know. The moment I was born, my grandmother stopped talking outside the house. Complained no more. She took a breath and something or other soothed her. Was it I? She fell asleep immediately. The woman who ought to be my mother, on the other hand, did not sleep; she gave me a look that ran over my body, anointed every component part with its respective name, turned me upside down with a feeling similar to tenderness, as nobody has ever looked at me since.

My grandmother looked at me disappointedly because I wasn't the boy she would have liked. My dad…he didn't look at me that day or any subsequent day, till I lost count. Then, when I stopped noticing he wasn't looking at me, he did look and did play with me. He was fantastic to play games with.

The girls had no idea about playing games. As a baby, she invented memories for me to send me to sleep. I remembered (played at remembering) how one of the two Esthers had played with me: at making tea, at mom and dad, at dolls, at whatever. She said that to soothe me while they lay their too-soft hands on me and sang out-of-tune songs. But I liked them a lot; not only did I doze off with them but when I woke up in the mornings my first thoughts were of those two, and when I left school it was no different. For most of my childhood.

Sometimes I hear them being chased and they're never caught. Or are they different ones? They shriek, are scared of what's chasing them. They run, fly, will do anything to make their escape. It must be other girls each night, must, it must be, because nobody could escape, lest anyone deceive themselves, it is impossible to escape. One night I shouted to the desperate one, but she didn't hear me. I prefer not to shout anymore, it makes no sense and makes me ill. I am ill. I'm so afraid. I'm so afraid and can't shout *Mom*. It's a cry I can't utter, because I don't possess that word.

I have other words alright. I have *trees*, I have *house*, clearly I have the word *fear*, and above all I have the word *ducksinthepark* because today that's what I want to tell you about.

Who can I tell about them? Who? Tonight out of darkness I'll create people I can tell.

Ducksinthepark, Dad…he used to take us. They prepared breakfast at home. Then he'd head for school, speaking about the usual, a harmless game, so he thought, but which I found violent and disturbing. "I'm not your Dad…I'm not your Dad…I'm a man who's going to steal you, a child-snatcher…a thief…I'll take you away and ask for money for you. If they don't pay up, I'll make mincemeat out of you." Then he and my sisters burst out laughing. They laughed and laughed, guffawed, relished it while I thought: "Mincemeat? Money? What on earth…what on earth are we made of?"

We'd go to the lake in Chapultepec. We had breakfast though we weren't hungry, pecking, here and there, like ducks, at what they'd put in the basket, and we covered our feet in mud, coating the two-toned (white, navy blue) pumps we wore to school.

At night I heard the steps that frightened me then, though I thought they were harmless and if at night they didn't let me sleep, by day I felt they were sweetly soothing, and I felt sleepy in Spanish and sleepy in Math, in English, in PE, in every subject...But it was a sweet sleep, a sleep that never hurt, a tentative sleep, fearful of me. Now it has won out and I know I'll never be able to wake up.

Dad took different routes to school. I never understood how on earth you got to school. The streets always made me dizzy, never accepted me as one of theirs. I never managed to outsmart them. Nor the city. But particularly not myself.

He would take a different route, tell us stories, crack jokes, and was hugely happy with the girls he looked on in every sense as his rightful daughters. And we all were.

At school...I never remember exactly how we reached school. Suddenly I was there. I guess I got awkwardly out of the car, queasily, feeling tremendously relieved because I had arrived despite the threats of that guy claiming he wasn't my father...I walked in, tried not to fall over my own knapsack and it was so noisy—so noisy, so much chatter! I don't remember that either, I imagine it, I must have been there...I remember lining up in our rows in the corridor, the daylight on our left flooding through the huge window, while someone we couldn't see prayed loudly, said things I never heard, and then saluting the flag, Mexicans ready for war, and something like, *like buds whose petals an icy wind does wither*…Enigmatic words equally as, or more, religious than the words that begin the day.

One day in the middle of break, Maria Enela (that was her name, was—or that's what I remember, and will stick with—Enela) invited me into the hencoop with her. There were no hens or remains of hens, I suspect it was one of the nuns' projects that hadn't taken root…an abandoned building, clean for some reason, dark and silent. I went in with her. Then the steps came close and she asked me: "What are those steps?"

"What do you think?' I replied, 'Nothing to worry…"

"You know what I'm talking about," she said, "you know very well. I'm being followed…They told me to ask you."

I was so scared I started to run out of the hencoop. Enela ran after me, calling my name loudly.

I ran out of the hencoop, but as soon as I looked up I stopped: the huge playground was empty. Could break have finished? I heard Enela's footsteps behind me, no longer chasing me, looking (like me) for the way to our room. Why was the playground empty? We went up (me first, Enela right on my heels) the stairs dividing us off from the way into the rooms and what we called the "grand playground:" a beautiful, meticulously cared for garden, lush, ever-green turf, surrounded by hydrangeas, to which we girls only had access on holidays. As I was saying, we went up the stairway with a volcanic stone wall (or floor) on its left, and I felt Enela turning around to look at the whole expanse of playground—to the back, the basketball courts, further down the training track: javelin, shot put, long and high jump runs (with a sawdust pit), and she said "There's nobody there." How come we hadn't heard the bell, the very loud, very strident bell ringing the end of break? I was afraid, Enela was afraid as well. I felt there was no sense in going on up the steps, what was the point. I turned around, avoiding Enela's gaze, and I saw them coming out from the left, from where the co-op's terrace blocked the volleyball courts from view, I saw girls swarming out, a gray swarm, an army of ants in gray sweaters, gray skirts with gray smocks emerging from the hullaballoo in the cafeteria...At the end of the stairs, rather than walk a bit to the left and go in through the corridor door, I turned right and ran down the other steps: there they all were, jammed together on the coop's terrace packing out the cafeteria, receiving prizes from the school co-op, the tickets the shop managed by the sixth-year girls had raffled, as they did every year, and that gave two girls carte blanche to eat whatever sweets they wanted from the co-op for the rest of the school year. Someone pulled at my sleeve and said: "You got one!" They pushed me to the front, to the co-op counter and I shouted my name. "Where are you?" shouted down one of the big girls from a towering height. "I'm here," I answered and they shouted my name, clapped, another big girl got hold of me, lifted me on the counter and there was a round of hurrahs and *vivas*, they hip-hip-hoorayed, gave me the token (a blue voucher, bearing my name), and then the bell rang to go back to class.

...like the girl on the terrace, for some time she's been chasing a lizard and finally grabs it, holds on and the lizard is *running*—how can it run if she's still holding it? She lets go of what she's holding: a tail dances a happy, triumphant dance on the ground, distracts her. How long was she rooted there? For longer than it took the lizard to scurry out of reach…Exactly the same happened to me with the voucher from the co-op. The time it took me to realize was the time it took me to find the classroom and meet Enela's gaze and decide that, at whatever cost, I must avoid her…I couldn't stand my own fear, a fear I reflected in her…

During break the next day I made quite sure I didn't go near Maria Enela. It wasn't easy, she cleverly wormed herself into the group I played games with.

When they went down to the playground areas, I didn't go with them. I waited till the last minute to go out in the corridor. I'm trying to remember the name of the girl who looked for something she'd never find in the bottom of her knapsack, stayed back for ages in the room to avoid showing the others her shame at going out by herself (again!) and wandered through the most forlorn corners in the school. She was chubby-cheeked, with a single plait of hair piled high and covered in lacquer. Of pale complexion, pinkish cheeks, she revealed a fragile spirit she'd never manage to hide, not even when she changed prematurely into a beautiful adolescent. I can't remember her name. I asked her to come out with me on that and other mornings when Enela was able to maintain her fleeting friendship of convenience (that nobody understood better than me) with my girlfriends; not many, but for me they were the longest mornings of my schooldays. Long, bright, too slow—what you might call "boring."

I wasn't bored. Sitting on the stairs shaped like a slice of watermelon for the youngest girls, we gossiped about this and that, swaying imperceptibly to and fro. We'd taken refuge in the children's playground, the one overlooking the kindergarten and, though it wasn't out of bounds, nobody used it, isolated as it was from the other playgrounds in a territory apart, and there we played a familiar game I knew well (because I played it unconsciously) when I was older: conversation. What did we tell each other? Many things, spelling things out as never before to anyone. Did you know that her Dad, that mine, that Esther, that the Spanish teacher, that... we gossiped like adolescents, like adult women, like old women, at length...

And so time went by between the encounter in the hencoop and the order I reclaimed stumbling in the darkness of fear. There were few nights when the steps didn't stubbornly pursue me, hiding behind the sounds I listened to as I tried to get to sleep.

That morning it looked as if it was about to rain. In fact a few drops did scatter the long line organized to play last girl out, and we rushed excitedly into the corridor between the classrooms to escape the rain. A good runner, I beat all my friends into the corridor. I came upon the following scene: they'd taken my older sister's satchel out of the classroom and were jumping up and down on it; as she tried to reclaim it, they applied to her Mom some adjectives I didn't understand... I thought about the glasses she used for reading the blackboard, they'd be reduced to pulp in the inside pocket of her leather satchel that still looked new before it suffered the downpour of kicks that crescendoed in harmony with the storm. I piled in after the satchel, bit the calf that in its turn jumped on top, bit deeper and deeper…they tried to pull me off her, but the rage I felt was such it wouldn't let me open my jaws as the leg's owner shrieked and the others shouted and my eyes shut. I remembered the satchel in my sisters' room the previous afternoon and thought it wasn't fair what they'd done to the satchel, and gripped my jaws tighter as the teacher pulled me by the hair, disheveled by so much scrimmaging and, in a deathly hush, took me straight to the office of the headmistress, Mother Michael.

I should have been afraid. I'd never been taken to the headmistress before, it was the last resort in the school discipline code. To start came the notes sent home, green (first warning), blue (second), and pink (third and final, almost a crack of the whip)— they all had to be returned to school the following day signed by both parents. If these notes weren't enough, there was the office, the scary interview with Mother Michael, which nobody ever talked about because it was in the realm of the *awesome*. I wasn't at all afraid of Mother Michael, of course I'd be incapable of disobeying her, of being rude toward her, but no way was I going to have consideration for anyone in the state I was in, seething with rage…I don't know how the teacher pulled me off without bringing a mouthful of flesh with me.

Mother Michael opened the door and started speaking. I told her about the glasses, the new satchel Esther had bought the previous afternoon, the incomprehensible words they shouted at my sister to define her Mom, repeating them singly, as I remembered them.

Mother Michael looked me straight in the eyes. "I'm going to have to punish you," she said, "otherwise all the girls will start biting their friends, but you did the right thing. Stay with me. Teacher, pink note for those who jumped on the satchel." I stayed with Mother Michael. No sooner had the teacher shut the door than she looked at me again, spoke to me in English, her mother tongue, for a long time, for a very long time, taking big strides as she paced up and down. I'd never known her so talkative and didn't understand what had made her like that. She left her office and left me there waiting for the home-bell.

Did I go to sleep in Mother Michael's office? The drawers in her enormous wooden bureau creaked *in a loud voice* when I was bored of waiting. They creaked and creaked, one by one, and right away I heard the same old footsteps inside her bureau, the steps that Enela mentioned sowed a seedbed of terror. I couldn't leave the office, I had to obey Mother Michael, I was trapped, the steps were there, next to my legs that hung limply from the chair, they'd come and I started crying telling them: "Alright, please don't make a sound, I'm afraid of you, please take Enela instead."

I don't know how I dared say that. The fear I felt is the only explanation.

The sound stopped immediately.

Next morning, after entering the classroom with my friends, under my desktop I found a message perched on my books. Who could have put it there? It was adult handwriting. Before I'd finished reading, I shut the desk, rolled the message into a ball and put it away in my knapsack. Could it have been my teacher? The footsteps again! Enela asked for permission to go to the bathroom and the teacher refused: "Go to the bathroom when you've just walked in?" *You sneak on Enela*...that was the first line of the message... *You sneak on Enela*...and the steps sounded in the classroom, nobody seemed to hear them except me and evidently Enela, a terrified Enela asking to go to the bathroom.

"Look, Miss!" shouted Rosi behind me. She pointed to a puddle on the classroom floor under Enela's desk. "Look..." Enela fainted, head on desk, skirt soaked, her eyes staring like a dead woman's. "Enela!" She didn't respond to the teacher's cry. "Rosi, run to nurse."

How did they take her out of the classroom? I didn't notice. She didn't come around. My head was spinning.

I didn't hear Dad's joke as he drove along. When I reached school, I got out of the car and waited impatiently for Enela. The day before, the school had called in her parents, who went to fetch her and take her home. I didn't think it would last. I promised myself I would be brave and talk to Enela about the footsteps. I spoke to her silently. I wasn't sure, perhaps we could oppose, even defeat, a fate I didn't fully understand but was beginning to glimpse desperately.

I waited for her on subsequent mornings. Enela never returned to school. I never dared ask teacher about her.

I tried to forget her and regretted not reading the message someone placed on the books I kept in my desk. I never found out how I lost the piece of paper. When I got home, I locked myself in my room to unfold and read it, but I couldn't find it, it was no longer in my knapsack. I was afraid I'd dropped it, that someone else would read it before I did and blame me in public for what I knew I was guilty of, because it was true. I had *sneaked on* Enela, but, why had I *felt the need* to sneak on her?

"*Looking at the lion, which he had been delivered over to like a young lamb, he replied:* 'What are you doing here, fierce beast? There's nothing in me that belongs to you; I'm going to Abraham's bosom where I'll be welcomed in a few moments.'

"*Suddenly his face glowed like an angel's. He went to his heels and rested like a dove by the soles of his feet. But the time to receive the reward for his labors had come. He began to feel great weakness and lack of strength and before the infidels' astonished eyes he passed over to a better life.*"

Mother Michael read with her strong accent in religious education class, the one subject for which she assumed personal responsibility. The headmistress shut the book of the lives of the saints and started to talk excitedly in her halfway language, mixing English and Spanish, exhorting us to think what a sacrifice the saint had made!

Well, I thought, I must be a coward. I sold out Enela, blabbed about Enela...I didn't need to compare myself to the flesh of the martyrs, as my schoolmates were doing, to know how puny I was...I didn't need to test myself in order to fail the test and know my shameful weaknesses. I felt more afraid than ever and the steps fed on my fear, ate into it, grew on it, swelled out, turned into the monument to the remorse-ridden cannon fodder I hadn't realized I'd become.

2

I never knew how I passed the end-of-year exams. If I were to try to endow my story with any kind of logic, I should describe how the Enela episode created real problems for me in my studies. Tormented, remorseful, guilty, punished merely for being who I was…I should have found it impossible to concentrate. But it was this inability to concentrate that earned me the merit medal, the prize awarded as first place for achievement.

I learned in a state of distraction. Learned what? Who knows! I don't remember a single word. I don't know what the subjects were. I was absolutely outside myself, who knows where, getting ten-out-of-ten in subjects as a result of not being anywhere, mentally skipping out, retreating to small islands that—as they didn't come from my imagination but from study plans concocted by bureaucrats—faded, leaving not even a trace I could cling to as I did at the time. The topics made me a Robinson Crusoe of unknown islands where I wandered, not sharing with anyone, not knowing how to return to familiar territory, islands that escaped the destructive hurricane that had devastated my world.

The "conquests" (if Crusoe ever conquered) brought me fame: a silver medal with the school shield engraved on one side, while on the other at the bottom it read *1963, third grade primary*, in the center my name and above it in big letters *Medal for Merit*.

I expected nothing. I had no idea of the value of the ten-out-of-tens I was getting, the fruit of my distraction. When I arrived home, my sisters made a big fuss, called Dad at the office, told Esther excitedly, repeatedly, what the ceremony had been like in an incessant bee-like hum, and Fina and Esther locked themselves in the parents' bedroom while Malena, the eldest— whose satchel I'd plucked from the stamping feet—took off my uniform, said loving things to me, dressed me in an elegant creamy pink English woolen suit (just right for winters in other continents but sweaty on sunny afternoons in the valley of Mexico), leather shoes...even put my socks on!...how grateful I was to her, every morning I sought out someone to help me do that because I hated doing it...She spoiled me like a young mother, combed and tidied my hair, made a bun, buffed my slides so they shone...She didn't remember her Mom—I never found out what happened to her— but she had learned to use herself as a substitute.

Esther and Fina had stored two wonderful surprises for me in Mom's closet: a heavy silver chain to carry the medal and a pair of white gloves made of fine, gauzy material: Esther's First Communion gloves.

Dad soon arrived with a strawberry cream-cake and a gallon of chocolate ice-cream. It was partytime.

Few days are as distant as that one! How I'd love to relive it! That day—a real pleasure—culminated in the tiptoeing on feathers that I'd invented from what they called "studies," and which only served to bewilder myself, forget myself, forget what I'd seen at school and at home, as I'll now relate. Under the layer of feathers you didn't have to be a princess to discover the green pea, but it was relaxing; even today I'd like to fall asleep reciting the names of capitals, dates of importance for the fatherland, biological processes, or *whatever* we studied with such apparent persistence, little pleasure, and total lack of interest.

After the round of private classes that Esther and Dad's trip to Brazil submitted us to (painting, dance, swimming, French) filling up our afternoons in their absence, and from the logical rebellion against any evening class we showed on their return, we made afternoons one never-ending roller-skating rink. Neither the precipitous rush down our street, the noise of the metal wheels, nor the constant falls brought on by our helter-skeltering made me feel insecure; I danced on them without moving, knowing that in the end the precipice constantly beckoning the tips of my toes remained under control and that the constant to-and-fro with myself wasn't from within myself: it gleamed righteously from the wheels of my skates.

By the side of the house, not on the immediate boundary to our land but a couple of houses further on, was scrubland where my sisters and I spent our afternoons. We lost ourselves, cut flowers that came with the rains: daisies, wild violets…sunflowers we never dared cut, they seemed as imposing as mammals.

I say *mammals* because being *animals* wouldn't be enough for them to defend themselves, insects are animals we attacked fearlessly, hunted down and used live (to play) or dead (jewels to be collected). Alive or dead they ended up pinned on the back of a biscuit box with Campeche wax.

We beat them to death: knocked them out with ether. Those that didn't die by this delicate means drowned in the sludgy soups we cooked in the holes we dug that would have honored any barbecue.

When the rains were over, they set fire to the scrubland. We witnessed the whole operation. My sisters were certain they saw escape rats, lizards, and (they said this, but I doubt it was true), snakes—vipers like the ones young kids sold from door to door, tied to a stick, tails of horses killed in mythic combat, because catching vipers was as easy as pie! They were capable of catching any animal, even monsters if necessary…

Malena and Fina shouted excitedly turning the conflagration into a source of pleasure. Transformed into a statue on skates with eyes that could see (note: could *see*, not imagine) faces in the flames come to observe me, bodiless faces, faces with all their features intact. One opened fleshy lips to call to me. Hearing my name they all smiled. Then their place was taken by a festively turbulent crowd eating *faces*, I saw it, I was there, it was not a creation of my imagination, and my sisters, tired of asking me to move away from the blaze approaching as quickly as the steps advancing yet *again*, came and dragged me away so the flames didn't devour my skirt or hair.

When I got home, they scolded me and put me in front of a mirror: my brows were singed, the eyelashes of one eye white, curled over, my skin burnt.

I thought I would stay that way, my face hairless.

"Looks like they over-singed her," said my adored grandmother when she saw me (fortunately!) that very afternoon. By causing a fuss I got her to invite me to sleep with her and they agreed because—as they said—"she's very on edge."

3

When I slept in Grandma's bed her heat helped defeat the darkness. We got into the same bed, were very close, and I smelled her, heard her breathe and felt the rhythm of her breathing was mine and, I wouldn't dare to vouch for this but I think it was so, I dreamed her dreams, rested from my own, from the savage disorder the world of my dreams inhabited whenever possible.

By her side I *slept*. I woke up after her, with daylight playfully bathing my eyes: nothing had called to me in the night, nothing had put me on alert, nothing had said *come*. I was left there unburdened, as I am now so far from myself. The sounds didn't brush against my shoulder.

By night I couldn't invent a code to group the terrifying sounds but I was collecting them, creating a dictionary without definitions, an auditory lexicon. There must surely be an appropriate term to call what I created out of the noises pursuing me in the night. But I didn't explain them: I never said, "That's the wardrobe door creaking," among other things, because I was also afraid of the right door to the wardrobe *just because I was*—because it was there, because it was by my right leg and I felt it was about to explode, scattering shrapnel of the unknown…I didn't put defining labels on the noises I could list because definitions wouldn't have helped at all, wouldn't have soothed or calmed me, would have only brought ingredients to swell the vein of fear. I would have been much more alarmed to know from where they came and how they developed!

There were those pursuing me more insistently, though they weren't the ones I most feared. I listened to them when those awake still meandered outside my bedroom; I didn't want them but they were beautiful, didn't let me sleep, had the constancy of a truth... They were noises produced by the wooden floor, insects hitting against the windows, golden or silver peals resounding off the walls, small steps taken in woven shoes, soft steps... All these were fine and homely.

Afterwards I fell asleep and the ones that woke me up... the ones that woke me up! I was in holy fear of them, a nameless, tasteless fear, a fear outside me, that went beyond me... They were perhaps vaguer but much more violent.

I have remembered them for quite some time, trying to distinguish which object they belonged to but I can't. I know them, I'm very close to them and haven't heard them again. I would have to see my house again to find the bit they came from—where, where, where, from which part they emerged to alert me, to make me understand they were for me, that they sounded for me, advancing in the darkness, groping here, there, colliding, yet not finding me.

I knew their blind hunt would finally not bear fruit. As they approached, though they brushed my neck or passed scarcely a foot away from my feet, though I could hear them and everything surrounding me was filled with them, they missed their target, the white target that was my heart before the shadows devoured it.

Why was my heart white? Two or three sentences are enough to relate how I had been pursued when I was just a defenseless girl waiting for them, unable to fend off that persecution! A few words easily define the whole restless night when they woke me in order to pen me in: "A frightened girl suffering nighttime panic because she hears menacing steps closing in on her in the dark." What is "closing in?" The question was never put, and it was never explained in a few words who "she" was...

I didn't know what I could do against this persecution. When I was younger, I stayed in bed or ran to my parents' bed to let them protect me, but Dad never let me sleep in their room, thinking my nighttime terror was "clowning," which was the word he used to describe it. Some nights I managed to trick them and stay asleep on a rug at the foot of their bed, thinking their closeness would defend me, but when I was older, let's say around the age of nine, I stopped having recourse to the rug; if I didn't stay in bed waiting for the noises to hit me I walked through the house trying to elude them.

Don't imagine that what I saw was producing the noise! The geography of the noise (the sound of crickets' wings rubbing, the dog's nightly walk across the grass, a pigeon stirring, cars speeding by in the street like a gust of wind, yucca leaves, curtains touched by mosquitoes), objects settling perhaps, or perhaps the odd one, that wasn't what I *saw*. I would like to have experienced the adventure as an explorer and discovered what could kill off my nighttime terrors.

The sonorous lexicon was only a small part of the non-verbal world I invented or inhabited as a child. What filtered through the sieve of words was the world I shared with the others: "Pass me the sugar, kick the ball to me, I'm cold, I want to eat, I want more dessert, I'm sleepy, I don't like the teacher, Gloria's my best friend, Ana Laura's the tallest in the class, how daintily she walks, I don't like going to Rosi's house, Tinina is very good at basketball, I like Dad pillow fighting with us. Esther: I don't like you shutting yourself up in your study, my sisters have another Mom who isn't Esther, nobody talks about her at home, her grandma doesn't like me, sometimes they go to see her, I heard that Dad pays my sisters' grandma's bills, the poor things, Esther took us to get our hair cut and left us in the beauty salon, the ladies chatted about things I never heard talked about at home, I'd like to have younger brothers, at school all the girls have little brothers, my collection of stickers is very small, my sisters' very large, I think the PE uniform is ridiculous, my bike's red, the building workers working on the corner sing all day, Inés made us orange jelly, I don't want to take sandwiches, I want to have school meals…"

The non-verbal universe was much more prolix, had many more inhabitants, situations, was much more worldly… A world without words corresponding to each word. *Scissors*, for example, what are scissors? Two knives living together, opposite, yet in apparent harmony.

I'm going to tell you about scissors. Young girls were not allowed; they were an object we couldn't touch. We only had access to pathetic scissors: blunt, stunted scissors with no point, wrongly called scissors.

Or in other words there were scissors and scissors. The first were adult weapons. They were for sewing, cutting material, hair… There were some dark gray ones in the kitchen—big, heavy, thick—so distinctive that on their account alone you could say there were scissors, scissors, and scissors.

The first were the ones Grandma used, those Mom used. You just had to grow up to have access to them. They were pale, shiny like the second pair (the "girls' scissors") and wore the mark of age—as if wrinkled—like the third.

The third pair lived in the kitchen. They were ownerless but had their uses: to cut chickens' necks, chickens' feet, to slice up meat to make stews. Not only was it totally forbidden for us to touch them, I wouldn't have wanted to use them: they disgusted me. Though they cleaned them, they were always dirty.

That night I was woken by different steps, more scraping sounds, light, dangerous. I could hear them coming from afar, something told me I had to stop them. I got out of bed and went toward them. Something dragged itself toward me over the wooden floor in the dining room. I wasn't afraid and went over: what was the turtle doing in the house? They'd brought her from Tabasco so Grandma could turn her into soup on Esther's birthday, and were keeping her on the kitchen terrace so the dog wouldn't bite her and she wouldn't bury herself, because we'd never find her to cook if she hid under the ground.

What was she doing there? She was running across the dining room (we children know turtles can run), she ran toward me, her heavy burden lightened by fear. They'd told me not to go near her, that she could bite me, futile advice because there was no way to get hold of her head; hairless, wrinkled, she hid it as soon as she sensed someone approaching.

She ran toward me, her head touching me as she reached my calves. I crouched down: her eyes bright with panic, she didn't call me by name, didn't shout for help, because turtles can't talk, that's the only reason why. I picked her up and held her to me, as heavy as she was, and could still hear the steps, the dangerous steps that must be stopped at all cost.

I walked through the dark clasping the turtle to my bosom like a defenseless lover, as terrified as I was, I said to her: "I'm going to look after you, don't worry." I stroked her shell with her head resting on my shoulder, stroked her rough feet that were too short, and we could no longer hear the noise we were pursuing. Not one step more. Confidently, feeling powerful, I took the turtle to the kitchen terrace. I opened the door, left her on the ground, soothed and I think also exhausted after her long run. I gave her a little water in a dish, shut the door and went back to bed, surrounded by a pleasant silence.

As soon as my head was on the pillow, I heard something strange and felt heavy breathing underneath it: I lifted it up. The vile scissors from the kitchen were under my pillow.

What were they doing there? I was afraid of them as children usually are afraid, a sensation I was almost unfamiliar with and I didn't know how to react. I picked them up with disgust, smelled their foul smell. I deliberated and decided to take them to the kitchen.

I don't know how I reached my decision, I don't know if I was more afraid of being scolded (I imagined the scene the next day: what were the scissors doing in my room?, a question they would ask rudely) or was afraid of scissors. I took them and put them back in their place, hanging from a nail on the kitchen wall. I was on my way back to my room and to bed when I heard the scraping steps again.

I understood too late. I ran into the kitchen but the deed was done: the door to the terrace was open, the turtle was bleeding and the guilty scissors, splayed out, leaving two trails of blood on the floor. The turtle was headless and missing a foot.

Horrified, I went back to bed and didn't cry because I was too afraid: who had repeatedly opened and shut the door? Who had left the scissors under my pillow and why? As on other nights, the quick beat of my heart lulled me.

The following morning I ran to the kitchen to see what they'd done with the turtle. I asked Inés the cook about the turtle and, as usual, she didn't answer. She carried on squeezing orange juice for breakfast as if nobody had spoken to her: in her book we girls didn't exist. We were things to be drilled into routine.

I tried to open the door to the terrace, but, of course, it was locked. Then Inés said: "Let the turtle be, you've been told it bites."

I waited for Esther to come out of the bathroom. Why did she take so long to wash? I reviewed her body parts wondering what she'd be soaping, she'd taken so long, but I had listed them all mentally by the time she opened the door. When she finally emerged wrapped in a towel, I asked her about the turtle:

"It must be out there."

"But is it?" I asked again.

"How can it not be there?" she responded. "There's no way it can escape."

I returned to the kitchen. The scissors hung dark and ominous

on their hook, while the cook kept her back turned to me.
I promised myself not to ask any more questions about the turtle.

We did have turtle soup on Esther's birthday. As I stirred my spoon,
I thought, "Which turtle went into this?" I couldn't resist, and,
breaking the promise I'd made to myself, I asked aloud:

"Which turtle went into this soup?"

"A river turtle," Grandma replied.

"I know it's from the river, but which turtle is it?"

Silence fell. They exchanged knowing smiles.

"One you didn't know," Esther told me.

"And the one here?" I asked.

"It escaped, nobody knows how," Esther answered.

"Why didn't you tell me?"

"You didn't ask."

"I did ask you one day."

"But it escaped after that. One day it didn't dawn here. It flew
off somehow."

She laughed. They all laughed around the table except for me.
I burst out crying. Out of control, I put my hair in the soup, in
the hateful plate of meat and plantains, in the green saucer that
till then I'd been very fond of.

While Esther said to me "Why are you crying? Come on, calm
down," my grandma thought she'd be cleverer and said, "She thinks
we're eating her turtle, the one that disappeared."

4

The holidays fade before the all-pervading start to the school year. It was 1964, we'd had very few days of classes, and were still in pursuit of the missing gadget, the book the school should order because it wasn't available in bookshops, and the wooden ruler that had taken us the length and breadth of the city to confirm its overwhelming defeat at the hands of the plastic ruler, an ignoble defeat lamented by Esther who described the winner as "rubbish," "gringo stuff."

I said that the holidays fade (though I don't forget them) because at the beginning of the school year it snowed while we slept, a real event in our temperate city. Esther woke us up. I stuck my forehead against the window, steaming it up as I watched the shapes of the plants in the garden sway tirelessly in the wind, being cloaked in deathly white.

What a magnificent silence! Esther, Fina, and Malena, wearing their dark overcoats over their pajamas, went out to touch the snow in the garden. They walked respectfully around the edge, teetered, ashamed they might sully the whiteness...What did they feel outside in the dark? I felt an ineffable peace in myself, silence at last, the silence I'd wanted all those years and which I'd thought impossible...

As soon as they came back in the power cable for the lights yielded to the unexpected weight of snow, fell, lashed, flashed, and sparked like an exhausted child embracing the eucalyptus that sheltered my sisters' games.

Only my sisters'. It pursued mine, tripped and tricked them. I had many such instances. For example: my sisters made necklaces from the top part of the eucalyptus seeds, or camphor as Inés called it, the part that, separated from the rest of the seed, looked like a tiny conically shaped cap. They put lots together, threaded and then painted them in bright colors. When I tried to thread them, they came apart: I could never put together a necklace or bracelet or even a ring, because the little caps disintegrated in my hands and became bits and pieces on their own.

I wasn't clumsy with my hands. With glue perhaps I was (I clearly remember some paper cows I was told to stick to a piece of white paper they handed out to practice my addition, which I brought back to school covered in dirty stains and thumbprints that struggled stupidly till they won out against cows seemingly unwilling to be made of paper, stuck down and imprisoned in the representation of adding-up sums), but I say *perhaps* because the majority of the tasks I invented at home, *provided I didn't do them within sight of the tree*, turned out perfect or, rather, to my liking.

I enjoyed sticking, trimming, threading, but really preferred running and chasing. This was the type of game the eucalyptus most sabotaged, there were few occasions I did (tried to do) my homework in the garden before finally taking a botched effort to my room or the kitchen.

The eucalyptus antagonized me in many ways: if when we played the tree was a neutral spot, what we called base, which if you touched you escaped being caught or were happy winners, I would lose for sure! Because when they reached the tree trunk and shouted out, they all realized *I hadn't touched base*—the tree had backed away from me.

Well, I know as well as you do that a tree can't move, that a tree has roots and is stuck there, but you don't know about a tree dead set on going against a girl. Imagine its leaves chorusing hatred and revenge. Imagine its roots determined to go on the offensive, its branches, its bark, its buds riven with anger! For that kind of tree anything is possible.

The tree always denied me shade. Even my sisters realized that, we'd sit and rest after playing (or collecting seeds from the tree, or looking for clover, or gathering mushrooms in the rainy season), and its shadow eluded me whenever I sought it: because the tree knew what I wanted, read my desires, and did all it could to frustrate me.

Yes, I'd sit in its shadow and, like a jealous sister, it pulled away, though its shadow belonged to the trunk's natural shape and that had to be broken by itself on the ground though it was painful and against its own interest to do so.

I was so aware of its attitude that one night, when I was sick and coughing, and Inés tried to give me tea made from camphor leaves to get me better, I refused to drink thinking it would give the tree its best opportunity to hurt me.

Because of what I've related, the sight of the electricity cable lacerating my enemy was a sign to match the happy silence, an omen that I took to augur a splendid new school year.

My fourth year at primary school was a fine one. But the silence ended with the snowstorm and the cable was removed from the tree the next day. It was a good year, but deceptive at the beginning, making me feel that I myself was no problem, that I was just like all the other girls (even a less likely target than the others), but the illusion was destroyed that Tuesday when I went into the bathroom halfway through a math lesson.

That was my mistake, my first mistake. I used to walk cautiously around school, I know I was totally vulnerable there, that it wasn't my terrain but territory I shared with six hundred girls. For me being careful meant belonging to a group, joining in the most energetic games, frantically trying to enjoy myself. During breaks, that is, in class, I listened to teacher. That did me more good.

But the Tuesday I'm telling you about, coming out of PE, I stayed so long at the water fountain that a long line formed behind me. We'd played volleyball—it was volleyball season at school—and in my enthusiasm I'd gotten sweatier than usual. I wanted to be on the team going to the championships. My throw was spectacular and I couldn't see why I wouldn't qualify, particularly if I entered into the training sessions as if my life depended on them, concentrating on the ball and on the gestures of the rival team as if I were two-eyed... I mean: as if my two eyes were autonomous and could look in different directions.

So I lingered at the water fountain. Drinking lots of water led to asking for permission to go to the toilet mid-lesson.

And, rashly, off I went.

5

Everyday my sisters and I wore the same underwear to school, the same gear from the same shop. Socks, panties, and vests times three justified Esther charging Grandma with the task of buying underwear on a special trip downtown: taking me by car, I don't remember who was driving (Grandma never learned how), to the

Liverpool Stores parking lot—the one with wooden benches on the pavement in the exit corridor, a premonition of the interminable wait for the car—and the walk from there to the usual shop to buy panties and vests on calle Uruguay: white cotton, with a pink, blue, or yellow bow to identify at a glance which of the three they belonged to.

It was a short walk to the shop, Grandma and I were very good walkers, she with her strong legs and a wide-eyed granddaughter to drag through the city streets, and me running in fits and starts: if we had to avoid, for example, the giant (a man on stilts, I think his name was Guama, at that time wandering long-haired and bespectacled on Condominio Insurgentes, where Grandma's doctor had his surgery practice), I hurried up; if I wanted more time to look at something or insisted she buy small donuts, or extra if she'd already bought me some, those they made in a side alley in the city center, their oily, vanilla smell impregnating our nostrils for whole blocks, I slowed down.

None of the to-and-fro characterizing our promenades could happen between the carpark and Cherem's shop because there were only clothes shops, identical in my eyes, "bad ones," according to Grandma, as a result we arrived at a military tilt compared to the endless time it took Grandma to choose the same underwear, the same as the previous year in other sizes, same designs, year after year exclaiming, "I'll take these," "Good quality cotton," or even, "How pretty" (that was excessive)—clothes Cherem packed in cardboard boxes every year while arguing over the discount with Grandma, who was bargaining passionately over the fixed 15%.

One day, I don't know how, I managed to persuade Grandma,

and I arrived home with three nylon petticoats. Who knows the wiles I employed to overcome her traditional stiffness and persuade her to yield to my base passions and frivolous leanings. In a flurry of childish flirtatiousness, the three girls celebrated with a fashion parade in front of the mirror in my sisters' room, where the three child models wore bows, hairstyles we thought out of this world, and the same white petticoats in different sizes.

The Tuesday I'm describing I wore the nylon petticoat rather than the traditional cotton vest and bow. I say all this so you can understand my story about what happened in the bathroom.

The school bathrooms were large and always clean. At the back was a huge mirror, to the left of the washbasins and to the right of the doors to the toilets. The way in from the classroom corridor looked on the wall of the first toilet; the door leading in from the kindergarten playground was always locked. To come in from one corridor you had to negotiate the wall to the first toilet on the left, and that's how you reached the toilets proper. To my surprise they weren't empty. Older girls (from the high school, not from primary, as I didn't recognize them) were playing war-games with wet balls of paper. When I walked in, they carried on. They didn't say hello or bother me, almost as if they hadn't seen me. Quietly I closed the toilet door, pulled down my panties, and sat down to have a pee. It wasn't unusual for me to pull them down so far that they rested on my shoes. That's why I'd sometimes get them wet on the floor when one of my sisters had just gotten out of the shower.

That wasn't the case now; the ground was dry. A hand came

under the closed toilet door and, catching me unawares, snatched my panties to hoots of laughter. I finished as quickly as I could, came out, and asked the big girls to give me my panties back. "Which ones?" they said. "Mine," I replied. "Those?" They pointed to the ceiling. Soaked balls of paper accompanied my soaking panties that were also stuck to the ceiling, as if it were ground where they'd been laid out to dry.

I said nothing. I decided to go back to class. "Don't try to blame us, or it'll be worse for you," said the dark-haired girl. The other was thinner and paler, with wispier hair that looked soft to touch, a pale chestnut color, down to her shoulders. "Don't even dream of blaming us," she warned.

Of course I wasn't going to blame them. I wanted to escape. Another of them was waiting on the way out, her eyes glinting, with a well-formed woman's body concealed under her school-girl sweater. "Where are you going?" she asked. "Back to class." "If you can!" the trio chorused. And they started chasing me. Of course, it wasn't difficult to catch me and…what did they do to me? They tickled me. If I'd always hated them, now they also made me hate myself because they exacted from my body frightened laughs that seemed happy and spontaneous, because even if they made me suffer I also got the painful feeling that it was *pleasant*. As best I could, I tried to wriggle free but the three big, excited girls caught me and kept a malevolent silence.

The balls of paper stuck to the ceiling started to fall. You had to side-step them to avoid slipping on the toilet floor.

One of the balls fell on my neck and ran down my back. I stopped paying attention to the three big girls. I felt my back was burning. I pushed it hard against the wall instinctively protecting myself, and the burning stopped.

I didn't see them leave. Without them the toilets seemed darker. I took my sweater off and pulled up my school blouse: by twisting my head, I could see my nylon petticoat in the mirror, burnt, a gaping hole revealing an expanse of back. As I pulled my blouse up, the soaking ball of paper fell heavily to the floor under the weight of trapped water. I straightened my clothes. I looked for my panties and couldn't find them on the ceiling or on the floor. I returned to my math class and tried to concentrate on fractions.

6

The petticoat carried the sore, the stigmata. The three big girls who had filled the toilets with light were angels: the pallid, rebellious angel; the dark angel of good; the one in the passageway was the guardian angel from Purgatory. My panties were the soul over which they fought their legendary battle. The water that had burnt my back was baptismal water, inflaming my faith, searing my body like a flame of divine wisdom…

Fine for me, the explanation wouldn't suffice at home to explain the hole in my petticoat. The missing panties could pass unnoticed, but the petticoat business was more complicated. At bathtime I threw it in the linen basket and hoped nobody would realize what was there, just like a dark-edged sore.

I was in luck. One set of panties less in a house like ours meant nothing, the explanation for the petticoat: that it had been ripped by the washing machine. Esther commented, "That's why you shouldn't buy nylon rubbish." I asked them to return the rubbish to me. I wanted to play with it. Wearing the petticoat back to front, shoulder in front, the stigmata was right where the Roman thrust his spear. I painted the edge of the hole with a dark pencil, and with a branch I created a crown of thorns with no thorns, I attempted a halo from a metal hanger but it wasn't any use because my sisters didn't want to play saints and martyrs.

I preferred the lives of saints they bought us at home to the comics (as we called the cartoon books and story magazines) that other girls used to read. On the other hand, my sisters reckoned they were boring, and as soon as they could, on the sly, they bought Dennis, Superman, little Heidis, titles banned from home, and didn't even read the front cover of the *Exemplary Lives.*

I devoured them. Not that I enjoyed them, I didn't at all, but I followed them passionately, as much or more than the other books Dad brought me.

As they had no other success at home, I lent them to Grandma after I'd read them. When I visited her, she'd read them to me again or retell me the stories: at stitch one Rita was confessing to her parents her desire to become religious; by stitch two they don't give her permission because they're old; by three she doesn't know whether to fulfill her desire or stick to her parents' wishes; by four she obeys her parents, back to stitch one where they marry her to a hard man who abuses and beats her; by two Rita doesn't lament, follows Jesus's advice and grins and bears it; by three he's also bad-tempered outside the house; by four he fights men from the village and they kill him; back to one. She was crocheting beautiful white tablecloths for when my sisters, cousins, and I got married. Although Grandma shared my admiration for the saints, I never thought of asking her to judge the stigmata the Romans had inflicted on my body, so after one boring game with my petticoat, I put it away in the drawer next to the colored pencils.

One day I tied it to a stick and made a tramp's bag to collect pebbles from the yard next door.

(I feel surrounded on all sides by loose ends of memories I've invoked when telling you my story. They all rush up, *want my hand*, as if they were children, shouting "me first," and I don't know which to take first, for fear that one will rush out, decide not to come back in a fit of pique. I lecture them: "Memories, be patient, let me take you one at a time to consider you more favorably, please understand that if you come at the right moment you'll shine better in my eyes, you'll burst and liberate all the treasures hiding on the backs of your roan mares."

Grasping a loose end to weave into the next story, the chosen memory then smiles. Which makes me happy! You'd think it loves me, that as it passes, courses through me, it feels affection for the girl who one day (when it participated in an anecdote) shaped it.

When I decided to tell you this, to invent you in order to tell this, and by having an interlocutor to have words myself, I didn't imagine the bliss my memories would bring. Though I can exaggerate slightly my epiphany, I might say I've come alive again.

The others, the memories I didn't choose to take their turn, fierce and faceless, sidle behind my back and mock the loneliness I inhabit, my opacity and my sadness. I'm not worried by their jokes because soon, if you're patient, they'll become generous smiles.

The enclosure I suffer I find *comforting*. I'd never have believed it! Comfortable, warm, propitious. Only here can I weave my story with such pleasure, without the memories breaking off when summoned, because only their pleasure *takes place*.

I'm sorry I can't retain in a single moment everything told here, can't feel in sequence everything I wanted to reach your ears!

Do you remember? With difficulty! For you, just one more story! So many to wile away your time with…I envy you. I only have memories and what I imagine I might have experienced between the memories.

If only I could write what I relate and devote eternity to reading it…)

The pebbles that I "collected" from the neighbors' yard were small, white, and were used by them to decorate the window box adorning the front of their house.

Collecting them was an adventure because they were just beyond our reach and because they were "cultivated" pebbles, "pedigree" pebbles and not stones from the street, so nobody should see us when we got them.

This wasn't difficult in our neighborhood.

Back home, we washed the pebbles, polished them with an old toothbrush, and used them to play with: tokens for snakes and ladders, to decorate school models. They forced me to repeat one piece of work because I took in geometric plasticine shapes (a blue cylinder, yellow tetrahedron or something similar, and a green cone) decorated with pebbles.

My schoolmistress must have found the inlay too eclectic: a woman with a mass of reddish hair and thick bangs who wore an enormous scrunchy the color of her dress on a ponytail drawn up on her crown.

She was stumpy (some sixth graders were her size), vigorous, and energetic. I can still remember the face she pulled when she saw the figures:

"What's happened to your work?" she half-complained, half-asked.

I couldn't see what had happened. "Did it get chicken pox or fall in a load of dirt on the way to school?" She accepted an illustration (even congratulated me on it), though it had Brasil with a *z* (obviously, the encyclopedias at home, written in English, printed it like that, though the *z* was all I got from them because reading them gave me a headache)...

The pebbles on the plasticine figures, on the other hand, were cruelly rejected: I had to throw them in the classroom trashcan at the teacher's insistence.

How humiliating! Those pebbles fished from next door's window box, carried in the depths of a holy petticoat, the source of so much happiness (the games I mentioned and a much bigger one I'll mention in a minute), had no future at school.

My sisters and I invented countries with the white pebbles: on the floor or in the garden we made maps of nonexistent lands, in the center of which we crowned each other, in elaborate ceremonies, queen of the countries they marked out. The crowns were gilt or silvery plastic wigs, inside which our heads sweated and enjoyed their trying beauty. Wearing Esther's high heels, we recited lofty hymns in praise of the modest fantasies of power we represented in our respective kingdoms. Never has there been such a resplendent coronation as the one when I was crowned queen of my own kingdom, perched on a rickety chair on my bed, wrapped in a sheet. With the pillows tied in a bow to my waist, my sisters had wrapped around my slender body an expanded dress without need of any crinoline. The nylon petticoat (a rag by this stage) hung down pretending to be the train of an imaginary gown. What glory was mine! From dizzying heights I contemplated the white frontiers of my territory, as much as the ample wig and my untidy fringe allowed me: the pebbles drew a misshapen *o* around the bed. Malena had asked Esther for shepherds from the Nativity: kneeling down below, their arms reached out in supplication toward me. Next to them two over-white ducks looked on respectfully, keeping close to the mirror from Esther's bag, a lake where the ducks would water their muddy lineage...

"Watch out!" "You'll fall off!" And so the game ended. I didn't in fact fall but stripped off my royal garments because Inés was calling us to the bathroom, and then in full domestic mode, we cooked *enfrijoladas* dowsed with cheese, stuffed with chicken.

They only removed the chair from the paraphernalia of my kingdom and made the bed; before going to sleep I restored some pebbles dislodged from their frontier. When I closed my eyes at the center of the territory edged by pebbles I noted the silence surrounding me, a silence tinged by a silence different to the quiet absence signaled by the snow's silence: I no longer heard the adults still wandering around the house or the noises that preceded the footsteps and echoed in the huge bell-jar of night...At the center of a territory invented by chance in a game I managed (finally!) to escape the painful darkness that closed in around me. The pedigree stones cared for me by silencing the house throughout the night so I might sleep. The pure habit (of the sounds) woke me in the early morning. The house was silent. I got out of bed and left my pebble boundary: the noise was there as usual, the steps and the sea-shell echo of fear continued their tireless activity. I jumped on the small island of silence and, in bed and happy, I closed my eyes. My nightmare had found its cure.

On subsequent nights, as you can imagine, I placed the white pebbles around my bed. I forgot everything else: cleaning my teeth, taking my work to school, putting laces in my shoes, answering question number four (or whatever) in an exam, but I never forgot my redeeming nightly boundary. I enjoyed myself in my paradise of silence, I let myself go like any girl in the simple pleasures of childhood, I changed tens into eights and sevens in my school notebook, dared to go to my girlfriends' houses if I was invited, and noticed how nobody at home was curious about my pebble boundary. Every morning, the cleaning maid swept them up and threw them in the trashcan. I was the only one they mattered to.

For a few days plucked at random from the calendar we three girls went to Cuernavaca, to a hotel described by Esther as *delightful*, called Los Amates because there were a couple of those enormous trees in the garden. A man called Don Alfredo managed the hotel, I never heard or have simply forgotten what his surname was.

The waiter who served us in the restaurant was called Primitivo, the rooms were small and uncomfortable, and despite the boiler the pool was never even lukewarm, but Esther was happy conversing interminably with the master of the hotel.

Don Alfredo wrote poems. One was to the weeping willows that could be seen from the terrace, others to the village where he had lived as a child. He'd been married to a Jewish woman, had separated (nobody ever said *divorced* in my house) at some time or another. He'd had a daughter by her who must be (or so Dad reckoned) more or less Esther's age.

My sisters and I ran on the grass, played cards, snakes and ladders, Monopoly, went in and out of the pool…did everything we could to break the thin veneer of tranquility over the place. The hotel never seemed to have guests. At night, although I alerted my practiced ear, like a bell in the darkness, only the wind could be heard, when there was one.

Nothing ever happened in Los Amates. That was guaranteed and that's probably why Esther chose it (underestimating the importance of her friendship with Don Alfredo). Nothing happened, nothing ever happened. Even the sun which at midday elsewhere in Cuernavaca seemed to burn down in a searing shaft of light, here its rays were bland, soft, askew, apparently fortuitous. But those three days a character turned up who was a stranger to our world, a girl Malena's age but already a woman, and I mean a woman gone rotten, not a mature woman: sad and perfumed like an overripe fruit, her eyes painted as if they'd spent more than enough time in front of the mirror, she smoked and her tender thirteen-year-old body wore her womanly attributes like trophies (I don't mean the trophies of big game-hunters but trophies as in *atrophied parts*): her breasts, long legs, waist, which at thirteen still hadn't taken shape, corresponded to those of a slightly overweight woman, not the uniformity befitting a girl's body. She wanted the world to believe she was a *frustrated* woman, when she was in fact rather a frustrated *girl*, a girl not kissed or caressed by her mom. (In the hotel parking lot I heard people say "She's the drunkard.") Over with before she'd grown up, she seemed to be searching: in fact she didn't want to find anything because she thought there was nothing to find, not even death.

One midday I went over to her while she was painting her nails irritably, like a woman bored and overfamiliar with the routine. I looked closely at her hands, muttered something or another and saw hands covered in varnish and her carelessly painted nails: she dabbed here and there, never quite hitting target.

"What are you doing?" I asked her.."You're not doing it right."

She stared at me, her beady eyes seemingly unable to focus on anything.

"Do you know what my name is?"

"Yes."

"And you do know what word's like my name, don't you?"

I didn't dare say no. Now, as I can't remember, it doesn't mean anything to me. Then she told me a joke about Christ on the cross and the Mary Magdalene woman doing something I didn't understand, and I didn't realize it was supposed to be amusing, and after laughing and forcing me to laugh with her, that look that transfixed me (a mongrel's, a roach's, a shitty fly's), she said:

"What do you know? You shouldn't even be asking me why I paint my nails that way, or can't you guess?"

If I didn't dare confess to her that her joke hadn't passed through the window of what my parents called my *innocence*, I did confess I didn't know why she made such a mess of painting her nails. "Don't you get it, or what?" She answered that it was—I can't remember the word she used— to deceive, so her hands couldn't be recognized, or that's what I understood, and I asked:

"Why don't you want to be recognized?"

Then she took hold of both my wrists and, pulling me toward her, raised her right hand and placed it on my girlish nipple, pushing aside my swimsuit to touch my skin. Gently pinching my nipple, she told me on the mouth, mouth to mouth, like a kiss of words: "I'm doing what I can to be saved." She separated herself from me.

My swimsuit strap had slipped off, I looked down and saw on my breast the red mark of nail varnish, over my heart, a new— brutal, painful—stigmata. Not one I wanted to preserve. I threw myself into the water and swam till no trace was left on my breasts of the red welt of pain left by her rough caress.

At the time the road from Mexico City to Cuernavaca seemed endless. Now, looking back, I realize it was short and easily definable. On that occasion when I traveled back, with Esther driving and the three of us happy to be going home, we all four sang while I thought: "What was she trying to tell me? What must she save herself from?" I took the mirror from Esther's handbag and looked at my face: dark eyes, clean skin, a face not like hers. Should I paint my nails?

I asked Esther: "Hey, Esther, will you paint my nails when we get home?"

"Little girls don't paint their nails."

"I don't know if they do, Esther, but I want to paint mine."

"It's not right."

"It's just…"

"No."

When Esther said "no" she managed to convince us more efficiently than any authoritarian mother, without making us lose face. "It damages the cuticles. And looks ugly. The varnish doesn't allow the nails to breathe. It's uncomfortable. It looks cheap. No."

And I said with her: "No, I shouldn't paint my nails."

As soon as we got home, I persuaded Malena to come and collect more pebbles from our neighbors' window box. I say persuaded because they were tired of the pebbles, and infatuated with a microscope for which they spent hours and hours gutting and slicing all there was to gut and slice and the stones, as they weren't looked at through a microscope, were no longer of interest.

They'd brought wonderful booty from Cuernavaca to dye and observe for days, and that's all they seemed interested in.

As generous as ever, Malena alone accompanied me, but. unfortunately for me, the trip was to no avail. The neighbors had removed the pebbles from their window box and taken away the earth and plant which decorated it.

A couple of construction workers were putting up scaffolding to drastically reshape what was quite a horrific façade.

I asked them about the pebbles. "Which ones?" they answered. Malena described them and they shrugged their shoulders, said they didn't have a clue. I went home distressed and fearful, while Malena tried to persuade me it wasn't so important and rehearsed the delights we'd see under the microscope.

Nighttimes sharpened their nails, returned to mock and pursue me.
I only had to close my eyes (not even go to sleep) and the noises and steps tormenting me increased in volume. Nothing could replace the protective impact of the pebbles. I tried various substitutes and was scolded for spilling hair cream, moth balls, rubber…I also set up a line of straws, biscuits, and my skates next to my sisters'.
All to no avail.

7

Grandma's telephone number was 16-19-50. Our house's was much simpler: 20-25-30. The numerical irregularity of Grandma's must be the reason why we always got it wrong when we tried to remember it, whether it was the housemaids, my sisters, or yours truly, who always thought she had a good memory. My sisters also vehemently maintained you had to look up Grandma's number in the yellow pages, which was always the preserve of businesses, industry, professionals, services, and products, while the white section was for private individuals. The vehemence with which my sisters defended consulting the yellow pages was due to a television advertisement, made with cartoons, as if for children.
The advertisements were enigmatic. While a female chorus

sang *"consult* (they paused here) *the yellow pages"* a single dramatic line linked Chinese restaurants with Quaker oats or any other chance coupling of elements, and their animated figures urged us to get the yellow pages, to use them whenever we had any telephone query though the extremely thin pages crumpled on hand contact, screwed up, tore. The commercials were not aimed at children and it was no surprise if their message went over our heads; nor did I ever understand the caricatures of Felix the cat, or—even less so—the tirades from a character called Chabelo, played by a big, fat adult actor, disguised as a child in shorts and Spanish-style sailor shirt, whining like a spoiled brat, showing off something that to my girlish eyes one should conceal at all cost even at the risk of seeming fatuous: stupidity. It wasn't just his dreadful patter, it was also the way he spoke, the clothes he wore...I didn't want to appear gauche and ridiculous like poor old Chabelo: this television anti-hero re-prioritized our longings, displaying the worse excesses of kids (he even belched in public!). If we watched him it was because he represented the defenseless child who could defend himself (because of his size), the silly kid who was loved because he was just that...It had nothing to do with any promised, sought-after world, I didn't think of him as nice, nor did I understand him, but, like many other children, I felt for his immense vulnerability and extraordinary flab that pore by pore said I'm a kid, I'm silly and want to be loved, and if you don't love me I'll give you *a thump.*

All this is prompted by a memory I want to recount. It belongs to a year before the incidents with the petticoat, the medal, and even the one with Enela, probably 1962.

One Sunday afternoon Juanita, who'd just started working at home, stayed with us while Esther and Dad went with an "intellectual" friend of theirs to see Manuel Capetillo fight a bull. That's what they said, "Don Pedro Vásquez Cisneros is an intellectual." I didn't understand what they meant: he wasn't a young man with his long grayish beard and unkempt hair, he'd sit and smoke his pipe in an armchair that otherwise had no presence in our house, it was only noteworthy when Don Pedro came to flaunt himself in his gray beret, which heaven knows why he never took off, perhaps because he was bald or because he could imagine how much we coveted it, although I doubt that because I don't think he had any intuition of us, we weren't at all important to him. Esther and Dad felt a burning affection for this "intellectual," pronounced with deep reverence his name and the label they'd assigned to him, and listened to him hold forth, open-mouthed, respectful, as if listening to a sermon in church. Shortly after his visits some blue stickers appeared on car windscreens with a drawing of a fish and the slogan *Christianity, yes, Communism, no* that someone had gone out of their way to plaster on shop and car windows.

I perceived in Esther and Dad's voices (I'm not sure about on their faces, they were parking the car and we were in the back seat), if not the same kind of admiration they felt for Vásquez Cisneros, certainly the same volume of admiration, when they spotted Elda Peralta coming out of the Elizondo bakery carrying her bag of bread, and the admiring tone was not for her (discreetly dressed in low shoes, a gray woolen skirt, a very light pink sweater, or so I thought, like any lady, like my Mom, not slimmer or taller, in a skirt that didn't allow her legs to open much but not so tight as to warrant small coquettish steps), but for the man she was linked to, a writer (called Spota?), one of those mythical beings whom Dad thought possessed the iron will he had always lacked to devote himself to the *humanities* as he would have liked, because his family persuaded him he must study something with an economic future, something to guarantee a seat at the banquet, at the *grande bouffe* the era would create from the magic of chemistry: chocolates made from next to nothing, jellies hardened by fresh air, sausage that never went bad, colorants and emulsifiers that enclosed in glass phials every possible tidbit, every morsel of food, mouthfuls of wealth, and not only that, also confidence in the abilities of men, intoxicated by a new renaissance that would poison the air, the rivers, the seas, the lungs of the workers in their industries, and, as if they weren't enough, those living in outlying towns and big cities. But before they realized their devastating impact, they copied patents and invented others to fill our hitherto pure air with a new nation...We didn't know then that fish were fleeing our rivers in search of water, their scales slimy with grease, that our jungles were cadavers of jungles, that the sea tossed detergent foam at the coast and dark patches of oil...

But I'm haranguing you with speeches that I've tried to understand and emulate, seduced by my visit to Raquel's house a long time ago, from the position I now occupy...I was contracted (in a manner of speaking) to her apartment. I felt so happy surrounded by books and pictures, by paper and notebooks, by dogs and the light that poured through the window!...Raquel would take her glasses off and on when she heard me walking near her till she stopped and looked up when she heard my footsteps..."Raquel Tibol!"

I called her by her first and last name. She didn't attach the least importance to my voice. That was when I was told to leave her apartment. Not that Raquel considered anything I'm telling you here. Her father was certainly not an industrialist and she wasn't worried by sand turning into chocolate or the bones of dead cows becoming sausages…But Raquel didn't find out about me *because she never stopped thinking.* I didn't want to deceive her as I don't want to deceive myself when telling you what happened at home that afternoon. We were playing in the garden as if the afternoon would never end— I felt no wind could disturb our *dolce far niente,* absorbed in a dragonfly, hanging iridescent, sometimes bluish, on the still air, accompanying us, fluttering her wings beautifully, motionless, chewing (as in chewing gum) its place in the fresh air of the garden, ruminating on the wing, as much a sister to us as we were to her— till my sisters took me away to watch television. We turned it on: the bullfight appeared, not from the seats where Esther and Dad were watching it, as tiny as everybody else, defeated by a paternal eye, by an all-powerful eye, distant or near, as it suited. The screen seemed it would burst from so many people, so many *olés,* so much overexcitement vibrating in the crowd.

However much I twisted it (my head, naturally, I wearied of looking at the ceiling and counting the blobs) I could find no better game than the boring search for Esther and Dad among the dots. But how could I know who they were? The television reproduced in black and white; Esther and Dad were not the only ones wearing hats, but all the heads showed up identically. I read repeatedly the advertisements on the barriers and would have preferred to do anything but sit watching television.

But we stayed in front of the television set, my sisters bored like me, and Juanita who I suppose was very young and white as a lizard's belly, fresh from the Opus Dei training school for domestics. Poor Juanita was a donkey (I can't really find a better word, or more measured term to describe her). She couldn't cook (in the training school she'd been convinced what she did in her house was not "cooking"), couldn't sweep, or so she said, because she wanted to use the vacuum cleaner in the garden and on the terrace, and revealed her character in a strange proclivity: she was fond of the mixer, which she would play with, empty, sitting there, relaxing, an oilskin top over the glass, yanking on the control handle to hear it "sing," as Juanita herself put it to me.

She *did* concentrate on the bullfight. Malena, Fina, and I— I don't know who started first— climbed a staircase of words escaping boredom like agile acrobats:

tequila

late

tea

ear

artistic

icthysaurus

usual

allow

owed

The last two letters of the word had to be the first two of another not previously used in the game. It was my turn to recite one that would begin in "ed" (it would have been *edify*) when I noticed how Juanita, quite unaware, was resting her hand on her

embroidery needle that they'd erroneously not expunged from her—
I mean the skill or the enthusiasm—in the "training" school classes.
I could clearly see the needle penetrating her skin and Juanita still
staring at the screen, her arm continuing to push her hand so the
needle went further in...

"Your go!"

"Your go!"

"Come on or you're out!"

I had to blurt out "Lift your hand up!" pointing at Juanita, as in
my view and my sisters' the needle slowly, inexorably kept going
in until it came out the other side of her clean palm, without
a spot of blood. Malena lifted Juanita's hand: a wooden palm,
covered in stucco: a saint, pierced, a needle transfixing incorporeal
flesh, engendered by abstinence, fasting, and hair shirts.

We rushed to the telephone to speak to Grandma, incorrectly
dialed *16-17-50*. A man answered, recriminated, told me to take
more care, a man with an opaque voice whom I guessed was fat,
heavy, and, no doubt, miserable. "I'm sorry." The argument started
with my sisters over whether we should look for the number in
the white or yellow pages, first carefully leafing through impossible
pages full of abbreviations: a coded language over which we argued
without a clue as to how it worked till in a temper we screwed
up and tore the inscrutable pages.

Juanita had followed us. In front of us she clenched the eye of
the needle between her teeth and pulled it out cleanly, as if it had
pierced material rather than entering flesh.

We three looked at each other, I swear with the same unblink-
ing look, parties to something beyond our understanding.

When Dad, Esther, and Don Pedro arrived, they found us washing in the tub (Malena and Fina were washing and doing my hair at the same time, trying to fix my soaking hair with some of the big, pink curlers Dad had brought Esther from the United States with the innovation that they avoided the use of hairgrips to keep them in place, since there was a kind of plastic mold in the same color to keep the hair shaped), while Juanita, in the kitchen, listened unthinkingly engrossed to her favorite concerto: suite for mixer and wooden table. We caused such a flood we almost wet Juanita's shoes without her even noticing.

The following morning, Esther packed Juanita off in the return bus to Michoacán to the same training school, surely to take more classes that would teach her to do nothing, to hold in contempt all that was her world with a greater degree of perfection.

8

My school motto was *serviam* (the hymn said: *serviam, forever serviam, though life may lead us faraway*). We were told ad nauseam that *serviam* meant serve, to work toward the glory and veneration of God, and to be of service to one's neighbor.

The word was written on the lower part of the school shield that lived with us daily on the white blouses and gray sweaters of our uniform: green and gold, embroidery thick like a growth, superimposed like a second heart of unerring goodness. It was at Esther's suggestion that they organized a drawing competition for possible interpretations of the school motto.

This wasn't Esther's first intervention; now, as on other occasions, she had interfered out of a sense of indignation: *las monjas*, the mothers, the sisters, or *las madres* (depending on who it was) had allowed a fifth-year teacher (my teacher) to set up a doll contest: the girl with the prettiest doll would win. The idea hugely annoyed Esther: Why reward something that didn't depend on a girl's will but was something brought from a shop? All the girls (except ourselves because we came empty-handed to signal Esther's protest) arrived with brand-new dolls competing with the most expensive, the one nobody had ever seen before, the doll from the most distant land with a designer brand.

The dolls were paraded before the eyes of the teachers who'd been elected as competition judges, who observed them perched on the hands of owners who'd never played with them, never changed their clothes, never cradled them, and never combed their hair so they would have a chance to win.

As an act of protest Esther proposed a competition in which the girls' skills would be valued and "not their parents' money or travels." She spoke to *la madre* Gabriela (being Cuban, she wasn't a Mother; being vigorous and intelligent, she wasn't a nun) and convinced her: "sensitivity," "intelligence," "work," "the value of work"—what other arguments did she use? I picked out these words from their conversation on the sunny terrace when Esther handed her a drawing that she gave as a present because she liked her so much: who knows how long they'd talked before I saw them, but they certainly loved each other dearly.

The graphic representation of *serviam* opened Esther's studio— for my sisters and me—on a single afternoon.

It was a spacious room. The light was what first caught your attention when you went in: a huge French window in the back, two skylights, windows on three walls, a large, vertical mirror—in which two people could be reflected if one stood on the other's head—as long as the wall and almost reaching the ceiling, bringing into the room a stream of light I would describe (now that I remember it) as *scientific*—a light seemingly able to illuminate anything. It smelled of eucalyptus branches, their transparent fragrance filling the open field of the room, the endless blue sky melding with our city air in the study, revealing volcanoes and mountains.

We'd never entered the study. I observed it with the same feeling I later observed a frog's heart in the live, open body of a drugged specimen in the school laboratory: I knew the heart existed, but seeing it—seeing it was something else. No fantasy was equal to the reality, no representation was an equal, ad nauseam I'd seen imitation (graphic, plastic) hearts as I had also seen photographs of Esther's studio, of fragments of Esther's studio, but they'd given me no idea what it would be like.

As if wanting to pluck out the gazes scavenging her bright study, Esther hurriedly produced big sheets of paper and endless packs of colors so we could draw what we thought denoted *serviam*.

In colors they never dreamed they'd have, my sisters recreated the houses that bordered on the school, the hovels of *la baranca* as the mothers called these settlements of "newcomers" to the city (some of whom were three times my age as they reached, tried to reach, the paradise they'd imagined the city to be) and drew uniformed girls, with big *serviam* shields gleaming on their chests, giving out sweets, injecting children or whatever other act they thought would heal or relieve the misery (like giving out *gansitos*, industrially produced cakes sold wrapped in cellophane bags, which was one of the drawings entered in the competition), while I couldn't outdo the light in the studio; leisurely, in ochre colors, I drew a small child, curled up like a baby but older, its body covered in *clavitos*, small nails, which would be small outside the proportions of the drawing, otherwise enormous hooks with nail heads sunk into its motionless body and face that if it didn't stop smiling, one could almost say it did. No tear, no wound, no sign of pain. Then I painted a bed behind him, a teddy bear, and a smiling sun that gleamed in the top part of the picture, almost burning the wings of some seagulls (or something resembling seagulls) flying past.

Underneath I wrote NAILS. Esther stood and looked. Said nothing.

"It's not for the *serviam* thing," I told her.

"I gathered that."

"A present for you."

She nailed it to the studio wall with a nail head identical to those in the drawing and kept looking as I hurriedly drew a girl washing dishes, the motto *serviam* enclosed in a bubble the edge of which was near her lips indicating the girl was saying the word *serviam* as she carried out her "Christian" action. This drawing on the sheet she'd given me was as ridiculous as all the competition entries if we stopped to think what washing dishes meant in our house that had a woman whose job it was to do it for us and whom I would never have been allowed to stop, what "helping" the *baranca* children meant when our very presence was an insult to them, what *serviam* and "to serve" meant if between us we made sure the whole country served us.

9

I wasn't a timid child. There are children afraid of anything and everything, of dangling their legs from chairs, for example, because they fear someone or something will grab them, or they're afraid of the shapes streetlights project from plants, plants already disturbing in themselves, changing shape in the dark, as alive as insects, or more so, shining like opaque jewels in the city night, swaying to and fro, scary; and there are children who are afraid of the dark because they just are, or who are afraid of being by themselves, of going to the bathroom by themselves, of walking around their home by themselves (let alone going out unaccompanied!), who are frightened in the cinema, frightened of going to the fair, who are terrified by the sight of a clown, who believe in child-snatchers…and there are also those who become frightened by dint of being filled with fear: the bogeyman, the devil, their dad, or, "Just you see what happens if…"

I didn't fit any of these descriptions. Things in themselves didn't frighten me, nor did they terrify me for no reason. I was brought up to laugh at, rather than fear bogeymen, witches, ghosts, the beyond. Of course, hell existed, but one didn't talk about it, it wasn't *probable*, it was something distant, too remote, and even impossible. The god in my house wasn't the god of fear but the god from another territory, I couldn't say its name or describe it because its geography and configuration vanished in my shadows. (I've just remembered one of the poems I learned as a child, my Dad gave us money if we memorized them, a peso a line, one that went, "My God I'm not moved to love you [one peso] by the heaven you've promised me [two pesos] or by the terror of hell [three pesos] to stop upsetting you…")

I could even say that not only was I not timid, but that I was brave. I remember one afternoon, to relate one instance, when I was alone in the garden while my sisters were setting up a game with Dad (I think it was called *the running heart*) that reproduced the circulation system with a pretend heart and veins, and while they were inserting tubes and sticking parts on the transparent heart, I—who never felt the least desire to play "putting-together" games, or even crosswords—I went out by myself to see if I could find a parakeet or something to play with. I stopped for a second and saw projected on the garden wall, right by the door onto the street, a vertical shadow, as if from the wall itself, where another small, amorphous shadow was going up and down, "It must," I thought, "be a cat going up and down…but where?" I never discovered what created that shape, what got in the way of the sun and painted the wall. Nothing, materially, could be projecting the vertical shadow, could be projecting the supposed cat that, without legs, ears, or tail (if you looked hard), was running over it. I slid my hand up and down, walked to and fro from the wall, trying to join my shadow. It was impossible. Nothing was creating that shadow. I wasn't scared because I saw it was completely harmless. It was still. It wasn't shaking, moving toward me, didn't want to hurt me. It was illogical for it to exist, it shouldn't be there, but I left it in peace thinking that, perhaps, it was also the victim of some persecution forcing it to project itself on a distant wall.

I sat down quietly to watch. Its shape didn't disturb me, it wasn't obscene, like the drawings I imagined formed by the stains from the floor-tile in the bathroom in Grandma's house, or those I carved in the dark when I couldn't sleep, obscene shapes with a solid mass and even breathing...

Why did I call them obscene shapes? What did I think obscenity was? Nothing resembling love or two bodies enjoying each other. Obscenity was for me the shapes added to bodies, deforming them, leaving them without fingers to touch with, lips for kissing, breasts to be caressed, legs or torso or the place where all that should be—it all projected shapes that frighten or try to frighten...Those were the obscene shapes that took possession of everything my eyes met when I was completely overawed by all that. I never see them. If they now appeared before me I would laugh myself silly. Because I'm not what I was like as a child. I am who I was, that's true, I am or think I have been the same from the day I was born to today, but my eyes are not the same. I've forced on myself the obscene task of deforming myself, of taking away my ability to embrace, to tear from myself the forms that hide a body.

I was talking about fear: nor was I afraid just after I discovered the attributes of Grandma's wardrobe, nor when I saw her upset and threatening me. Oh! That wardrobe could have changed the animated life of any household and would have done so in Grandma's, if she hadn't chained it up as if she were chaining a wild dog on the strongest possible leash for a piece of furniture in its condition:

used only as decoration, the wardrobe was an empty piece of furniture, full of absolutely nothing, clean, exasperatingly clean, like everything inhabiting the house on the Santa María estate.

I got to know the wardrobe's "wiles" one boring afternoon when traipsing around Grandma's house while she was engaged in an interminable conversation. Out of pure boredom I marked with a pen the pocket of the jacket I was wearing, not realizing my naughtiness, completely unaware, an unpremeditated act.

Before Grandma hung up I realized what I'd done. I took my jacket off and my nails scratched at the lines on the blazer material to try to remove the marks: small, inky blobs, bloated with ink from my ballpoint pen, running in lines, like rays from the sun, but dark. I looked at the little balls with legs and thought: "They look like spiders," I folded my jacket and put it in the useless wardrobe. At home they might not scold me, perhaps Esther wouldn't even notice, but Grandma would place great importance on the destruction of an imported jacket.

Grandma put the telephone down. "We must run." I don't know where, I don't remember where she was going to take me. Before getting ready to go out, she washed my hands and face, combed my hair, and ordered me to put my jacket on. I went to take it out of the wardrobe neatly folded up, telling her I wasn't at all cold, that I was very hot. "Put it on so you look nice." I put it on in front of her while she praised it because it was made in Spain, "Nothing beats Spanish clothes." I was expecting her to spot the stains any moment and to launch into a fierce scolding when her expression changed: gazing in astonishment at my body, she quickly took off her short-sleeved, done-up-at-the-front white smock that she wore to work in the laboratory in order to keep her clothes clean (although I never saw a mark on her impeccably-white coat), she held it like a rag and started hitting me with a corner of the smock, beating me, landing blows, and I couldn't understand what was happening...She scared me, but I wasn't afraid. I cried tears and shouted at the sight of my grandma not managing to articulate a word, red, but not in anger, beating her granddaughter with a rag, unflinching...I never imagined she was hitting me because she was angry with the marks, because nobody ever hit me as a form of coercion. Why then was she flourishing the overall rag against my body and why so furiously, so venomously? She was beside herself, the room bathed by the curtain of tears before my eyes seemed beside itself, and my shocked heart was beside itself...

She stopped hitting me and showed me, not saying a word, shaking them with the cloth, what she attempted (fortunately) to extinguish or stifle: the lives of four black spiders, fat, as if they'd been injected with ink. By shaking off their corpses and wiping a damp cloth over them, my jacket became clean, no marks of spiders nor ink.

It didn't make me scared of the wardrobe, nor did I ever think I'd see Grandma in that state again. I calmly took time to think it over: what wasn't that piece of furniture capable of? How easy it was to get Grandma going!

Now, am I easily scared? Yes, in a thousand ways. For example? I'd not be able, not be brave enough to repeat what I experienced as a girl. My memories make me fearful, and undermine the serenity of memory...

I didn't lie when I assured you it was a pleasure to have recourse in memories. It's true even if it scares me. I wouldn't dare live through what I experienced as a child because, once recollected, the facts turn into dangerous needles that could sew up my heart, sear my soul, and turn my soul into strips of dead flesh. As we live we hardly realize that we are alive... To relive what we've seen by the lucid light of memory would be unbearable and, as far as I'm concerned, I wouldn't be brave enough.

Fine then, but am I afraid of fantasizing? Instead of remembering, I could fantasize, imagine memories, falsify images and events. I haven't done so—everything I've told you was real, I haven't invented a single word; I've written my descriptions trying as much as possible sticking to the facts. Of course, I could have used more appropriate wording than those in the narrative I've been spinning (I did try to correct some, others I left because I couldn't find any better ones for my story), but I've kept to the truth, everything told here happened in my school, at home, in the city I inhabited and which may still exist, I don't know, maybe the city has changed appearance, has abandoned its young, clean, and biblically virginal face.

But there'd be no point in imagining. Either I overcome the fear I feel (and enjoy the pleasure) remembering and shaping the words that describe my memories, or I keep quiet. What's the point of fantasies, imaginings, lies...I can't see the point, it wouldn't give me any pleasure, and what if I were also frightened by what my imagination produced, if I had an imagination? If I had one, because there's nothing left in me. I am only an ounce of flesh that memories keep from rotting, from being consumed by maggots and flies, from final extinction.

10

When describing the world of my dreams to you a short while ago, I said the *savage disorder the world of my dreams inhabited.* Why use the word *savage?* I might have said *battered, violent,* or *sad* but the definition of the disordered world of my dreams would have been vague, and the word *savage* in the two meanings I encountered as a girl seemed a perfect fit: savages were the inhabitants of distant lands who behaved so much differently than ourselves (like my dreams, populated by hunting parties, burials, naked people running through jungle or desert, houses that had nothing in common with ours, inhuman rites), and savage meant also violent, destructive, capable of putting an end to everything.

Of course not all my dreams were the same. Their savage disorder might stem from a variety of actions, from diverse situations. For example:

I was walking alone across a huge park, down wide dirt paths. Despite the trees, I could see the brilliant bright blue sky, an explosion of light. Nobody seemed worried by the vulnerability of a girl in a white dress walking alone. I wasn't either. Confronted by a tray of cakes offered by a gentleman in a hat, I took a copper coin from my dress pocket and bought a sweet. As my mouth closed around the cake and I licked the first ball of fried dough, caramel-coated and hollow, night fell suddenly and with a vengeance; though it was illumined by high lamps like small suns switched on by an invisible hand, an all-embracing darkness threatened. The sweet was very hard, I couldn't break a chunk off, taking a bite only hurt my teeth, but I kept biting deep. I walked on and came upon a fountain, its vertical jet of rebellious water surging white and high into the air from round volcanic stone. Rain started to pour down. The jet continued its usual trajectory, as the rainwater scattered, gray, turbid puddles darkening the park. The rain disintegrated the cake I was trying to hold onto, dissolved it first into a rubbery mass and then took it from me and handed it over to the earth. The man with the tray ran by: it no longer carried tidbits, but *Nails*: that girl (or boy) I'd painted with a wound and given Esther as a present.

Where the uneven earth had formed potholes, where if I'd put my feet in any one I'd have soaked my shoes and socks, jets of water began to rise up identical to the huge fountain's, but in proportion to the water in each pothole. The rain was such that the water from the central fountain began to spill over the ground creating more and more puddles, each of them reproducing the form and mechanics of the jet of water, tiny fountains without stone parapets. Each jet reflected the lights in the park and there were so many that the ground seemed illuminated, full of immense stars. I felt there was nowhere to step, the ground was the sky and a sun would never again lighten the gray stormy sky to guide my feet away from the depths of night.

One of the small fountains spurted and wet my skirt and panties: I felt it was deliberate and silenced it under the sole of my foot.

Then the rain abated. The fountains in the ground stopped, were once more inert puddles, and the huge fountain in the park also began to fizzle out. I walked over to the fountain: colored salamanders were running across it, uttering words I couldn't understand, till they jumped out of the water, extending their wings, and disappeared into the dark sky which devoured them and left the park in the purest silence: now there were no passers-by, no sellers, not even the sound of water, nor leaves or rats who pattered here and there unseen. I too—I felt this distinctly—gradually disappeared, let myself be swamped by the darkness. Last to go were my eyes: I saw the park being snuffed out and—I'm not sure, but perhaps— perhaps it left the dream with me.

Why did I tell you a dream? I ought not to disrupt the flow of my narrative. I plucked the word *dream* out of the air because I want to tell you how it happened that from one day to the next I stopped dreaming: I never dreamed another dream again.

It wasn't long after I lost the white healing stones from our neighbors' window-box and after the four fat spiders ran down the jacket I'd painted them onto just because they spent a short while in an empty wardrobe, when one night, looking for a rational way out from my fear, I decided to demand white pebbles from the wardrobe. I quietly fell asleep mentally rehearsing how I would paint them so they resembled the ones I needed, recalling what they were like, trying to recall where exactly the light reflected on their tiny surface, following my painting teacher's advice (a bald, sometimes bespectacled man, I reckoned he only wanted to ask me whether I was Esther's daughter, his big toad eyes looked at me amazed and incredulous as I answered I was, I was, I was).The next day (there were no classes, or it was the weekend, a fiesta or the holidays, I can't remember, the more I provoke my memory, the less I remember) I asked to be taken to Grandma's. Once I'd arrived, I stuck by her side, started drawing, and as a result Grandma never stopped saying, "Just like your mommy," completely ignoring me and my drawings, as she was absorbed by the work in her laboratory (which was called Laboratorios Velásquez Canseco and developed natural raw materials for use in perfumes). First I painted a lonely pebble and colored it with my white crayon, so the sheet looked practically empty.Then, I drew a small heap of white stones. I took the piece of paper to the wardrobe and waited, sitting next to it on the icy, exaggeratedly clean mosaic tiles. Sitting there I remembered when a nanny looked after me at Grandma's, when they operated on Esther's eyes because, someone said, she saw "with difficulty"…My uncle Gustavo whistled by, dearest Uncle Gustavo, Esther's younger brother, and crouched next to me patting me on the head:"It's like a coconut shell," he said of my hair, repeating his usual joke. But I couldn't laugh with him as usual, I felt as if I'd gotten a stomachache.The brilliantine was still damp on Gustavo's freshly combed hair; he got up—as engrossed in his own world as I was in mine—and left without a word of goodbye, perfuming his path as he went. I heard him rush through the house and close the wooden front door. He immediately unlocked it and shouted from outside, "I'm off now, Mom," slamming the door behind him. I then put my hand in the wardrobe and took out the white pebbles and white sheets of paper, completely unmarked. I kept them all in a bundle in the pocket of my dress.

As soon as I got home I inspected them slowly: in effect, the paper showed no sign it had been drawn on; the pebbles were like the previous ones, as if the wardrobe had read the intention behind my drawings and ignored my clumsy squiggles. I thanked its generosity. Only the biggest stone, the one I'd painted by itself on a single sheet, was more opaque, not at all translucent and, no doubt, too white. I told myself that the wardrobe had also used it as a trial run, and put it away in the drawer where I kept my erasers, pencil sharpeners, dry leaves, packets of jelly, treasures I cherished but never dared to share with anyone, except, naturally, my two sisters.

Before going to sleep, when they switched off the light and thought I was well away, I placed the rest of the pebbles around my bed. I fell asleep very peacefully, it was true, undisturbed by the usual sounds of that time of night. Soon after the steps, the familiar sounds woke me up, which I greeted more startled than ever, principally because I had complete faith in the protective circle of white pebbles, they would cut me off from them, never thinking for a moment that wouldn't happen; and second because I felt *I hadn't slept*: I had dreamed nothing, nothing. From the moment I shut my eyes to the moment I reopened them, nothing passed before them: the film of my dreams had been wiped.

I never dreamed again. The steps kept resounding, perhaps more clearly, certainly hit a more fragile, more visible target; even asleep, I had no place to hide. Who had shut the doors? It was then I understood things aren't always what they seem, that it would be easy to recover what one sees, yet impossible to recover it in all its substance.

I never again arranged the pebbles around my bed. Super-stitiously, I resolved to collect them up in the morning and I gradually got rid of them one at a time, in a place from which I thought they'd never come back to haunt me. "Things aren't what they seem." Not always. You will understand I never returned to the wardrobe—if things within the order of their own creation rebelled and enemies found (if they existed) levers of support in there to bolster them or provide stations for what I initially called persecution, what would happen with things I'd provoked into existence? Just imagine! They'd already deprived me of my dreams, delivered me to the night, scalped, with fear my only shelter. What would other objects be capable of? I mean the things provoked, dragged by my willpower out of the nothingness that engulfed them.

And so if I was the only one who, by chance, had discovered the potential of the beautiful, carved wooden wardrobe, I kept the secret to myself.

It didn't take any effort.

II

"Malena! Fina!" I ran into the house, shouting to them. "Malena! Fina!" "That's strange," I thought, "odd they're not answering." They were so loving and attentive toward me. "Malena! Fina!" I asked Inés, and she just shrugged her shoulders. I asked Salustia: she stopped ironing, wet the iron again, waved a damp finger, and said, silencing the noise of the iron's contact with the water,

"They're in their bedroom."

I ran to their room. By now I'd forgotten what I wanted to show or tell them but I kept calling out. "Malena! Fina!" Couldn't they hear me? I reached their room: the door was shut. I tried to turn the doorknob, it was locked by the button you could press inside the room (something implicitly forbidden, nobody locked their door). I hammered on the door with my fist. "Coming," the two chorused. Their voices sounded different. What was this "*Coming*"? They'd never used that tone with me.

"*Coming*," they said, but didn't open the door. I started to hop around in circles, even forgot what I was doing there, but the closed door reminded me. I knocked again, they didn't answer. I sat down on the wooden trunk that had always been next to their door. I could hear them talking in the distance, whispering. I heard them say words I couldn't catch, that, for the first time, they kept out of my range. They talked and talked. Laughed. Walked from one side of the room to another, and every one of their actions underlined the one they were avoiding: letting me in.

Annoyed, I lifted the lid to the trunk. It was full of handwritten and painted notebooks, embroidered in Esther's warm hand and the drawings and paintings we'd always known from her. A small nail (like the one I'd painted) was in the center of a white sheet with no commentary. I put them back after reading a couple of lines I didn't understand. I tidied them and shut the trunk. Then (at last!) my sisters opened the door, silently observed me from a room that was no longer familiar, owners of a new complicity that had erased me, that had no room for me. On the bed lay an object that (more resistant than a lock, stronger than a chain, higher than the highest wall) had succeeded in separating me from my two sisters: a white object, folded in four, displayed on the quilt, which needed only candles to emphasize the sudden veneration my sisters felt for it. I asked them (in pure gaucherie), "What's the matter? Why wouldn't you let me in?" and they laughed between gritted teeth, looked at each other, making me feel totally unimportant. I caught another glimpse of the white intruder on the bed, noticed the straps and metal clasps. "What's that?" I asked. They ignored me as before, or, rather, (why lie, this is the truth), mimicked my voice, and mocked my awkward question. My hand closed in on the white enemy. "Don't touch," "It's not for children, it's for *señoritas*." I took a closer look: yes, I knew what it was, it was a bra like Esther's, I had seen them in the laundry room. But how did you wear them?

That was the end of our afternoons together, and I couldn't understand why. One night, a few days after, I went into their room as usual: Malena, not noticing my presence, was pulling on a nylon stocking as she stroked her leg, touching it like the statue of a saint, acting as if it were the leg of a *señorita*. Suddenly she saw me watching her: "What are you doing here? Go out and knock on the door before you come in." I turned around and rushed to shed some tears on my pillow, though warm (the grief springs from that temperature), icy in relation to the pain. I cried over the lack of attention from the two fairy godmothers who had protected the threshold of my being, had prevented monsters coming in from the outside, not realizing that what I should have been mourning was the *disappearance* of the girls who once had been my sisters.

A few days later we went camping with the guides, the female equivalent of the scouts (boy explorers) founded by a gentleman by the name of Baden Powell, a hero similar to Chabelo in my girlish eyes who dressed as a boy (in the organization's manual illustrations he came dressed in bermudas, neckerchief, and ridiculous hat, a similar outfit to the boy scouts), and who inspired courage in us during the nights in camp, nights when we went to sleep in the countryside and fought off what they wanted to be our routines and talents in childhood: from cleaning our teeth and washing to obeying our parents, sitting (*comme il faut*) in uncomfortable chairs, in uncomfortable armchairs, eating at uncomfortable tables, sleeping between uncomfortable sheets...We let our bodies enjoy the fresh air, in our view in total disarray and, according to our organizers' criteria, following the framework of a formative discipline, which fortunately none of us could feel.

This time we camped without tents on a farm. We stayed in empty, luminous galleries. My sisters avoided my company. I stayed at the back and saw them enter the next gallery, with a narrow, communicating door. I spread around the dry pine branches piled about to cushion my sleep and put my sleeping bag down next to nobody in the middle of the cement floor. I put down my sea-blue backpack as a pillow and when I raised my eyes saddened by a sisterly rejection that I now believed to be definitive I saw I was surrounded by an infinity of sleeping bags: there were no cement spaces in the gallery not carpeted by girls and their respective packs in orderly rows and a disorderly trail of dry pine branches that brigades of older girls swept up.

At night, in a scene lit by our battery torches, most girls laughed at Susana Campuzano's baby-doll outfit (a very short nightdress with matching panties)—she had positioned herself to my right to sleep and at that moment was making her triumphal entry into the gallery, tripping indiscreetly between the lines of sleeping bags, because, being timid, and experiencing the same age of transition as my sisters, she had gone to change her clothes in the dark countryside so nobody saw anything while all the rest of us mortals made a great play of taking our clothes off at the same time as we put others on in Houdiniesque contortions, given that our bodies were temples of the Holy Spirit to be seen by no one…she bounced in cheekily with her ridiculous, miniscule, nearly see-through nightwear, letting out short, sharp cries pretending to be imperceptible to denote shyness, when in reality she was continuously seeking attention, provoking a round of girlish ribaldry at the self-advertisement of her womanly body.

By the time she reached me, she'd stopped shouting. She slowed down and her two sad, blue eyes stared at me. She clambered into her sleeping bag. I saw her untidy hair slashed, the way many women treat their hair, irregularly, not able to fall naturally, almost mannish, but long enough to be pained by the shortness. I felt sorry for her. Then I thought how she certainly had wanted to hide her body from the gazes of the other girls, because I thought she must be ashamed it was no longer a girl's body, and I thought of my sisters and felt sorry for them, and sorry for Esther, and I thought of Dad, felt sorry because I remembered only men go to war, and thought "How are we going to manage to hide him when they come to take him to the front?" and then stopped thinking about that as I said to myself, "But there is no war, though what if one breaks out?"

Once more, I caught sight of the girl beside me. She turned toward me when she felt my gaze spying on her. "Hey," I said, wanting to be nice, sincerely moved by the situation. "I understand you, it's happening to my sisters as well."

"What is?" she retorted very prickly.

I kept a prudent silence because I wouldn't have known what to say to her.

Then I was the one who turned over and thought: "This will never happen to me, I won't let it," and, thinking that, I fell asleep, not realizing my wishful fantasy would contribute to my own damnation.

12

We were having breakfast. I clearly heard something drop into our garden. In a loud voice I said I'd seen something drop down as if it had been hurled in from the street, but nobody believed me. They were right to a point: I hadn't seen anything fall. I'd heard it fall so clearly that I could almost imagine the shape of the thing. I quickly finished breakfast and went into the garden by myself, running to the end under one side of the breakfast room.

Something had fallen inside the garden, as if hurled by the paper-boy and it had flown over the wall. I'd been wrong about its shape, what shone out on the lawn was something small, flat, and light.

It shone and was beautiful: a gilt, plastic frame surrounded the luminous landscape on the shores of a metallic blue sea, a metallic blue sea with scrolls and button roses, and a fake gold-plated wooden frame. In the background, the mountains and between the mountains and the sea a village—but a European settlement, not a South American village—all on shiny paper, like chocolate wrapping paper, what we call *orito*—gold foil. A few women strolled along the seashore, or apparently enjoyed sitting on the quayside. Nobody was working. The windows in the little white houses were open and every little corner gleamed.

Nobody swam in the water, but two launches waited for passengers. In another, a white-haired man was fishing, alone, not wearing a hat.

In the lower right corner it said *Razier*. Naturally, I hung the picture in my room, next to the dressing table, to the left of the mirror. Who would see it? My sisters, I've already told you, didn't join in my games anymore. Esther had her head in the clouds and Dad worked as never before. Neither of them asked me about the picture.

"Where did you get that from?" Inés asked when she saw it.

"I found it lying in the garden."

"You expect me to believe that?"

"Really," I insisted, "really, it was lying in the grass."

"Who'd ever throw away such a pretty picture?"

She stood looking at it, weighed it up like I did, and thought like me it was a place worth getting to know. And I said: "Would you like to go there?"

She didn't answer my question. Her face hardened and she turned her head but avoided looking me in the eye, and said: "I'd never go anywhere God hadn't made."

By a long shot, English class was the most entertaining in the whole school. Not having to restrict themselves to their academic duties, the level of English in the school being higher than the level required by the school authorities, the teachers let their imaginations fly, allowed us to work on projects in the library, go to museums, watch films, do a little bit of all the things they liked to do. As the holidays were approaching, Janet thought we could search the school atlases and encyclopedias for the place we'd like to go to. We could give free rein to our fantasies. Well, even the moon was possible if someone thought it would be a good place to go. Then we had to write in English the reasons for our choice, including all the data we collected, in our "research paper."

Where do you think I wanted to go? To the place portrayed in the picture, of course. I looked for it in the atlas, on the globe of the world, in a beautiful volume of *National Geographic*, on a huge map of Europe hanging on one of the walls in the library. Not a trace. "Probably doesn't even exist," I thought. But I couldn't believe it was an imaginary place. I looked in the *Encyclopedia Britannica*: its name and history were there. I went weak reading it, but what would I put in my project, if I didn't read it? The fact it was in English was what made it most tedious: it was forbidden to copy out sentences word for word, frowned upon even more so if one didn't attempt an original essay. My difficulty came on both sides: first, understanding it in English, then turning it into Spanish in my head, then turning it all back into English from a mother tongue base that I really didn't like to detach myself from.

I asked the library nun for help. She had a name I can't remember, something elephantine or so I thought. She didn't speak a scrap of Spanish. I said to her, "Could you help me find this name in the *Espasa Calpe*?" It was such a big encyclopedia that knowledge of the alphabet wasn't enough to track something down. The nun helped me find it. It was a very large entry. Before disappearing in the middle of the tenth century…Or in other words it was a city that no longer existed that had gone up in flames after religious conflicts and after it was repeatedly punished for serving as a bed of heresy.

The day after I took my picture into school and showed it to Janet. I explained in my clumsy English that it had been thrown (I didn't say to me, I said into the courtyard) and told her it was a place that no longer existed. "*Extrahno*," she commented in her dreadful Spanish accent. That was it. She advised me to keep the picture in my knapsack so as not to distract my friends. *Extrahno.* That was all I got for sharing something of my own with other people. I wanted, intended her—friendly and apparently interested in her pupils' work—to give me a hand with it, to find out who might have thrown the picture into my house and why. It was an omen. I knew it was: to represent a persecuted, ill-treated, and, finally one night, torched village, a night when most of its inhabitants perished in the collective bonfire, to represent that, I'm saying, as a tranquil holiday resort using bright shiny paper to do so, could only be the product of some malevolent will.

At that time I gave up the last activity I held in common with my sisters: our afternoon trips to the supermarket, because I was afraid of the few people walking around the area: building workers, plumbers, maids who didn't sleep at their bosses'. One of them had thrown the picture—had thrown it *to me*—as a warning I couldn't disentangle.

I know now that it was all just a mistake. The village or the name they had given the place had nothing to do with me, but what it experienced because of where it hung next to my dressing table mirror did—that really did have something to do with me.

Could there be icy looks that touch inert threads and fray them into raw nerves like people who awaken unrequited passions? Because the icy look from Janet, my English teacher, might have awoken the inert plastic, metallic paper the way I'll now recount.

Inés was combing my hair that morning because Ophelia, the young girl who dressed us in the morning, had gone to her village for her sister's wedding. She pulled at my hair as if I couldn't feel anything, as if my hairy hide were oilskin, insensitive or unresponsive. She combed as my two sisters hovered around her, explaining why Malena wanted her bows changed for two smaller, less garish ones, an explanation like throwing coffee into the sea because Inés didn't pay the least attention. I looked a little to the left of the mirror, to the place where the picture hung, the Razier foil portrait. Something exceptional, rather opaque, caught my attention, not like the rest of the picture, something dark and opaque, something that wasn't there before that looked like splashes, but splashes of what? Splashes of what?

Inés finished my hair and left without saying *be careful.* My sisters stayed, but nowhere in particular because they couldn't see me— I no longer existed for them.

I went over to the picture and, yes, it was marked and only

marked on the skirts the women wore, irregular, completely different stains, stupidly located, but always on the garments worn by
the women. I saw one with a brighter, almost shiny stain, spread-
ing over her garments as if growing from behind the picture...
I couldn't check or find out what happened because they shouted
it was time for me to get in the car to go to school.

When I came back, the picture wasn't in its place. I never
found it.

13

The persecution intensified. Used new wiles. I realized I could
no longer escape, I knew so at night as I tried to avoid it, and
remember it was so by day.

Luckily the school year ended and for some reason (doubly
good luck) Esther and Dad decided to send the three of us sepa-
rately on holiday outside Mexico on an exchange program pro-
moted by the Catholic association.

My destination was Quebec: in that city I lived in a family
with a daughter my age who was all for spending her holidays
the following year with us in Mexico City.

Uncle Gustavo drove me to the airport, and even accompanied
me to my seat in the airplane, visibly agitated by the sight of his
girl traveling alone. He gave me an impossible amount of advice
I could never retain and asked me (over and over again) to bring
him a bottle of Chivas Regal.

Inside my overcoat that was suffocatingly hot and uncomfortably big, made for a much bigger bear than me, I looked down happily on the clouds beneath, thinking that what was constantly on my heels would have to wait a couple of months or—best case scenario—abandon the chase.

There's practically nothing to tell you about the journey. I have tried to leave out of my narrative all the anecdotes that didn't directly lead to this point. I've in no way related what was my whole story. This conversation has been a selection, a gentle trawl so you know —as much as I do myself—about who I am, so you can accompany me as you listen and help me understand how if in this darkness there are no external bounds then perhaps they exist within the shadows shaping it. For example, I myself certainly have a form within the formlessness, or that's what I'm trying to affirm through this narrative. If I left out many years and many facts, I also erased from these words many people I associated with, mentioning only those who helped (all quite unawares) to bring me here, with the exception of dear Uncle Gustavo. If I didn't talk more about him it was because you'd have then understood mine was a different story, or even that I was a different person, but if I don't leave him out entirely, if I fleetingly mentioned his name, it was because in any re-telling I could never entirely erase him from my memory.

I will only relate one Quebec anecdote, memorable for two reasons that I'll combine. One was there at the start and the other arose later. I went to eat in the house of some of Esther's friends (or acquaintances or colleagues, I never clearly understood what linked them) and, seated at their tables, I really had a clear sense that I was hearing the steps and the noises I know so well, the ones that pursued me at home, but now at midday as we sat down to eat.

I felt so frightened thinking they had tracked me down, that this was the definitive call, that they knew how to ensure I didn't escape, that I had to stop eating because I couldn't swallow a mouthful, rather, I couldn't pass through my gullet the single mouthful I took of the roast meat specially cooked for my visit.

The whole wide world seemed to collapse like the extraordinary waterfall we passed in order to reach their house, the Montmerency falls, that I remember from the mute, single piece of evidence I preserved by mistake from the world I inhabited as a child.

Right here:

I ripped it from my holiday scrapbook to make more space for photos of my hosts and left it loose in no particular place, which is why it sometimes appeared in a notebook, sometimes on top of the desk, sometimes inside a folder. I don't know why I held it tight the night they came for me and didn't let it go. Here it is. It's the only thing I knew I had: nothing at all, a spurt of water in the darkness that by trying to remember so hard I've erased completely. I don't know what colors were there, it's black and white like the photograph you can see. I don't know what it smelled of, what its temperature was, if there was noise or silence. Nothing at all. Water, sky, trees, electricity or telephone cables—perhaps carrying voices that I sense and try to recreate—murky constructions, all wrapped in the same senselessness: What was the water like? Was it a violent, extraordinary descent, pure death, or was it lake water, quiet, peaceful, serene, like a tender mother, but gentler, more welcoming, no doubt more faithful, more protective?

And what were the trees like? Gently surrounded by leaves, cruelly protruding, sharp-pointed, rough, bare branches, or dead on their feet?

I had to say I felt sick at the Winograds. I couldn't swallow anything and my head was spinning. They lay me on a sofa while I listened to them chatting in the *quebecoise* I'd already got used to listening to and only half grasped. There I realized the steps weren't pursuing me, that they weren't after me and realized in the end, by fine-tuning my inner ear in my stillness, that they were following the only daughter of the house. Her name was Miriam. She was much older than me and was quietly humming a pop song as she looked at me out of the corner of her eye. I was doubly relieved; because I wasn't the sought-after prey and because of Miriam's attitude: the company of the noise didn't seem to upset her. She asked in relaxed fashion, making me smell cotton wool soaked in alcohol, whether I felt well and would like *un chocolat, un caramel, quelque chose…*

As soon as I returned to Mexico, I realized the territory I'd lost on my journey was perhaps greater than what would have been snatched from me if I hadn't gone away, feeling the millimeters of loss night after night as a tragedy. If before I left I thought I'd barely any territory left to defend on my return I just crossed my arms and waited for a rapid denouement. Panicking, naturally. I wasn't Miriam.

My house was never as big as it was then. I walked around some nights when everyone was asleep, tiptoeing, ducking under tables, looking for the equivalent of the well of eternal youth, El Dorado, the philosopher's stone, and not in broad expanses of uninhabited territory and on horseback, but on a carpet, under furniture, next to the pictures painted by the painters whose names I'll never be able to forget and who lived on the walls of our house—Fernando García Ponce, Lilia Carrillo, Manuel Felguérez, Juan Soriano—people who at the time were the painters of my city, and who had swapped paintings with Esther so each could have their own collection.

I brushed against furniture, climbed on armchairs, kept my distance from walls, made futile gestures trying to distract them and myself.

There were few parts of the house I didn't visit by night: the utility room, the patio, the terrace, the garden, and of course, Esther's studio, which I didn't visit by day either. I'd never been back there since the *serviam* competition, since I'd painted that figure that I'd baptized *Nails*. Why did I return that night? Because when I put my ear to the door I realized I could hear nothing inside, which meant I'd be safe inside. I thought, "They won't dare go in here."

I opened the door to the studio; dark, under a starry sky, it was really beautiful. A full moon, as perfect as in her drawings, its round, innocent face smiling down at me, I took another step inside and a shadow jumped (jumped!) out of the dark.

It was Esther. "Oh!" she spluttered. I stood watching her. She seemed younger than by day in a thin cotton nightdress, her face without makeup and her long hair loose.

"What are you doing here?" she asked. I'd liked to have explained, to have told her once and for all about the crazy race I'd become embroiled in, but I didn't have time.

"What are those noises?" she asked. They flocked into the room. Clung to the walls where I saw them, as if I'd caught glimpses of fragments of them before, I saw them bound to each other, creating the puzzle to that day I'd not understood, the fragments congealed around the *Nails* that Esther kept framed, hanging on the studio wall.

"But what is it?" she shouted or something similar as she rushed to protect me. All those things on the wall turned on her enraged, feeling disturbed, wounded in their hidden selves, began to separate out, bits of some from bits of others, bits of others from bits of others, till they formed a mass of fragments I knew so well. The pursuers set upon her. I took her hand and said, "Run, Esther, come on..."

"Please say Mom at least now!" she shouted in a panicky voice. "But what is this!?" she kept shouting as I tried to save her, I had been the one who'd drawn the pack to her study, till I heard Dad shout, "But what is this!?" and I saw Esther wasn't depending on my hand anymore, that I was by myself dodging them in the lounge, and I ran to my bed and cried and cried still hearing them and listening to Dad calling the doctor and then the shrill, deafening, strident, blinding call of the ambulance. I peered out of the door and saw two nurses carrying Esther on a stretcher. Esther (can I say Mom at this point in the story?) turned her head around to see me. I ran after her. The stretcher-bearers stopped. Her head turned around, lips half-open, she said, "Poor little thing," and burst into tears as well; oh Esther, I loved you so much, so much, Mom, Mom, Mom, Mom…

The hospital had strict visiting hours. We couldn't see her in hospital because Dad decided we should go to school as normal.

The doctors didn't understand her symptoms: she was seeing images in reverse (not all the time, but suddenly they'd volteface), hearing a constant thud, vomiting uncontrollably—and it all lasted three days before she died of what they diagnosed in the post-mortem as a brain tumor.

Dad insisted on her body lying at home. I couldn't stand it. Now I was afraid of Esther as well. Amid all the steps, I made out hers in the slippers she wore around the house, trailing them in her usual manner. One night I even thought I saw her in her pink flannel dressing gown coming toward me until just as she was about to touch my shoulder I shouted from within my dream: "No! No!…" Dad ran into my room.

"What's the matter?"

"I was dreaming."

Why didn't I go with her? She wouldn't have saved my life, of course, no need to say I'd have lost that with her as well, but what is the point of thinking about that now. It's too late, too late for me to regret anything, anything at all.

14

Although I almost never liked going to play in my girlfriends' houses I accepted Edna's invitation because the oppression I felt at home from the ebullient steps, sated on Esther's body, bloated and arrogant, was veined in sadness. We arrived (I wasn't the only guest) and they decided we were going to swim in their pool. Edna lent me a swimsuit. Maite, Rosi, Tinina, and Edna chatted as they took their clothes off. I didn't know what to do. I held the swimsuit between my palms like an altar boy and distractedly looked at the garden through the window.

"Don't you like it?" asked Edna. "Shall I give you another costume?" "No I like it, I'm off to the bathroom," I replied, or something to that effect. I shut the door in order to change and heard them continue their conversation. In a flash I heaped my uniform on the ground and slipped on the swimsuit. I went out with my clothes in a ball under my arm; I was embarrassed to find a pretty young girl in the mirror. I tried to catch the familiar look sunk between the eyebrows: I met a pair of cat's eyes. I drew my face back: a cat's face. I stepped back to the wall to see as much of myself as possible in the mirror: I managed to check myself out from head to shin, a pretty girl who set off walking to the pool.

Someone pushed me, two timid hands on my waist and I fell in, barely clearing the side of the pool. I opened my eyes under the water, clean and glinting, rippling, waving and pulsating gently like a huge heart: tum, tum, tum…I tried to propel myself and felt my body burning, felt my body about to burn up, and felt the water wouldn't allow me to strike out to reach the surface.

I stretched out my hand and grabbed onto a rung of the bars. I gripped tight, closing my stinging, blinking eyes in the water and when I opened them I looked at the boys' shoes. One of them most have thrown me in.

Edna handed me a towel. "You didn't even wet your hair," she said in amazement. "How did you fall in?" "Did you dive in on purpose?" "Did you hurt yourself?" "Did you hurt yourself?" The boys stayed silent. Nobody looked as if they'd pushed me in. I touched my hair: it was dry, totally dry, as neat and tidy as I'd just seen it in the mirror, parted down the center and the ends slightly shaped toward my body.

"That's Jaime, my brother, José Luis Valenzuela, the Cyclone, Manuel Barragán."

"Pleased to meet you."

"Let's get changed."

I wanted to go home. I telephoned. Only Inés was in. I'd have to wait.

There was something in the garden I couldn't understand, something I couldn't hear although it was pursuing me. I took my time changing, but they waited for me. Something was trying to undermine me. We sat on the bed to chat as I pulled my socks on. I looked up, searching for my shoes and took the opportunity to glance into the garden. I heard laughter. "It's my sister, the cocky one," Edna said. The laughter entered the room next door, crossed over and out into the passageway and stopped opposite the door. They opened without knocking.

The Angel from Purgatory and the Good Angel stood there, wearing the same uniform they'd worn that morning in the bathroom. The Good Angel said: "Don't shut yourself inside, girls." They turned around and walked on.

"Who's that?"

"Cristina. She's a bore. Let's go outside, she keeps whining to Mom. When I've got girlfriends in the house, she doesn't like me being with them in my room."

We went out and bumped into her Mom in the passage. She was wearing a clasp that held her hair slightly loose on the nape of her neck, and she stopped herself with both hands on both walls in the passage…She was wearing canvas shoes and dragged them lightly as she walked. She didn't say hello to us.

The sound of those steps was like the sound of Esther's slippers. I should have left Edna's house as quickly as possible. We walked by her mom as Edna gave explanations she didn't listen to: "We're going out…we were getting changed."

The boys were waiting for us in the garden. The two Angels showed no sign of life.

Dusk was falling, and my distracted self would have liked to be in the sun about to set. It had been decided we'd play hide and seek in couples. Manuel Barragán said *come on* to me and started to run. We hid behind some volcanic rocks while waiting a safe amount of time before trying to touch base, and there he asked, sticking a *v* for victory sign under my nose: "Do you know what this is?" and I answered, because who at that time among us didn't understand that obscene gesture: "You're painting violins for me." (What did "painting violins" mean?)

He was emboldened by the fact I recognized the sign. He took me by the hand to run together, a damp, clumsy cold-fingered extremity, something terrifying. I pulled on him to stop. "Let me see your hand," was all I could think of saying to him. He showed it me. It was a hand but in my hand his hand was a deformed cudgel, something rough covered in skin, an icy, jagged hook wanting to gut me. He pulled at me again to get me to run. What was undermining me in the garden? By the time I'd realized that, he'd pressed his face against mine and a thick, clumsy, cold tongue was trying to sink itself between my lips.

I started running toward the house. It wasn't that the kiss frightened me. I can say I had wanted someone to kiss me (out of curiosity, to see what it was like), but his stony-cold hand and icy face did terrify me. How could his body temperature be cold and the icy pool like a geyser? I started running to clear myself of the garden.

When I went in the house, I found the Good Angel sitting in an armchair with a man who seemed as handsome as a fairy-tale prince. One of them asked me: "Is something wrong?"

I told them I didn't want to be in the garden. "I don't like being in the garden either. They designed it so nobody feels at ease there," added the Good Angel looking at her boyfriend. "Now you've seen what Mom's like. Sit down with us."

I sat on a stool.

"When are they coming to fetch you?"

I thought I must be in their way. They were beautiful and seemed in love.

"Woyteh, do you know whose daughter she is? Esther de la Fuente's."

"Really?"

Prince Woyteh opened his eyes.

"Yes," I said.

"We admired her very much," Cristina added.

"Thank you."

"There are three of you, aren't there?"

"Yes."

"Was she good to you?"

"Very good."

"Didn't you resent the fact she worked? Didn't you feel abandoned because she worked?"

As if that worried me.

"Of course not!"

"Do you see, Woyteh? Of course one can. One can have children, have a home, and have a profession."

"Of course one can," I said, not wanting to be contrary. I didn't understand what she was talking about.

Fortunately the boy who opened their door came to tell the Good Angel they'd come to fetch me. "Excuse me. Thank you." Woyteh's hand wasn't cold—it was a *hand*, a hand identical in my palm to mine. Cristina accompanied me to the door. She was radiant. She opened the door and as if it were a condition to meet before she'd allow me to leave asked me again: "Can one really?" Instead of the hurried "yes" that I answered in my desire to flee this house, if I'd had the courage I'd have answered her: "Good Angel, do you remember how you bullied me in the bathroom at school?"

I got into the car and said hello to Dad with two syllables that he reduced to one in reply. Dad didn't add anything nor did I.

Well, the syllables were nothing to him and me alone, alone in this huge car. Not even the car spoke! It drove along silently, as if it wasn't touching the roadway.

Dad must have been very sad. I was very sad and disturbed, startled by Edna's garden, Manuel Barragán's icy tongue, and the conversation with the Good Angel. That's why I broke the silence.

"Dad, let's move houses."

"Why?"

"So we're less sad."

"We would be sadder."

We went silent again. When we went under the light from a streetlamp I made out some blisters on my small knees. I revisited them in the next pool of light. Touched my chest: it was burning. My neck was burning as well. The water in the swimming pool, the cold water in the pool had burnt my skin. On the other hand, the boy—who no doubt must have had a skin temperature of 98 degrees Fahrenheit if not more from the excitement of his adventure—had seemed cold. I went over it again and again, rocked my thoughts in the to-and-fro of the car. And so, my skin peeling, the pursuing spirits would have finished me off me that night. I needed air. I wanted to shout or cry and I spoke:

"I'm afraid at night…"

"Of what?"

"Of…" (Where could I start?) "…of Esther." (How silly, how could I say this to him!?)

We were going down Avenida Reforma. The car hit the right side of the street. He braked and started to cry. I stroked his head and he shook it to get rid of my hand.

"How can you be afraid of Esther? She's your Mom!" he was still crying and I didn't know what to do. "Don't you remember her? Would she be capable of hurting you?"

"Sorry Dad, I said something stupid."

"Besides, why do you want to leave the house? It was Esther's house. It's the only thing of hers I've got left."

He leant his forehead on the steering wheel and went on crying till I felt that his lament was so intense it could—like Christ's tears—save the world.

When he finished he mopped himself with his handkerchief and took me for an ice cream at the Dairy Queen.

15

Two or three days after the visit to Edna's, Yolanda and Vira, two of Esther's friends, the kind who argued for hours with her over their open books, came around to take the three of us to Bellas Artes. Malena and Fina were upset by the thought of this excursion. On the other hand, I'd had an excellent time when I'd been taken before. I enjoyed the music. I remembered the last time I went with Esther and Dad, years ago.

A Concert at the Bellas Artes...a night of music...how can I capture it for you...these scraps of sentences are not all purely whimsical!...My blue corduroy suit, the rabbit's fur brushing my chin, the shiny shoes...the whole night for us, not (as usual) merely a sleeping bag to wrap us in before sending us to sleep like chickens stuck on a spit...and then the music!...angel steps...pure

beings moving effortlessly across the ground, and if they were
flying it wasn't upwards, it wasn't to leave but to observe...they
were offering pure love there!...affection without bodies...nerves
without flesh...raw, painless nerves feeling...the luxury of enjoy-
ment doesn't destroy, drag away, snatch, transport: it keeps one
seated in the stalls...and how I wanted to dance!...I thought
I was dancing among them...the applause, then the excited listening to so much applause thinking everyone had felt what
I felt, that finally I had *communed*...leaving, crossing over...walking
between so many lights as on a stage, the pristine stairs inviting
exciting slides, the ceiling as high as a church, but joyful...listen
to the music...everyone be at the ready! Imagine yourselves in
the stalls: you'll be carried aloft by the notes to the edge of the
precipice, to a flight apparently trying to self-destruct, rising up
only to self-destruct...with what innocence my girlish soul sur-
rendered to the lilt of the music on that never-to-be-forgotten
night...If only they'd known how much the tiny spectator was
swept up with them, in what ways, how much I remained faithful
to them...loving, entirely theirs, my only body the one musician
and strings granted me...oh! If only I could remember, relive the
resonance of that music, how the sounds wove together, and fell
pleasurably to corrupt the soul...

I was asleep when we got home. They dressed my sleeping
form in my pajamas. In the night when I woke up near dawn
and heard the usual noises, I measured the poverty of what drew
near: their sounds weren't sweet, weren't harsh either, and carried
no musical sign. They were sounds without a soul, unfeeling, that
of themselves opened no doors, meant nothing. I was angry that

what pursued me bore no resemblance to the paradise I wanted as mine, I felt ashamed at the pettiness of what was avid for me. If I'd thought then that this world was awaiting me, known that this was the world *after* me, I'd have cried and cried, perhaps, till my dying day, I'd never have stopped…

Thus when Yolanda and Vira came for us and asked if we wanted to go to Bellas Artes, however much I shouted *please please please*, my sisters won the battle. Let's go somewhere else more fun. They took us to the cinema to see a film about men and women who lived in the future, in a modern world, who burnt the books they found because they considered them harmful. It had a hero, a heroine, an old woman who let herself be burnt by the flames in order to die with her books. From there they took us for dinner, but I didn't want dinner, I felt sick, I didn't know what from but I felt strange.

I asked for a dish with three scoops of ice cream, cream, and jam, and it was allowed. My sisters ate something or another and all heatedly debated the film.

16

I would like to finish my story here. The memory of a Bellas Artes concert, the aspirations I nurtured for a life of the emotions, the fantasy of having within my body a heart pumping blood and able to change its rhythm to act in step with the feeling of others, a heart that danced, able to listen, to fuse with other rhythms as it did on that occasion with the music…I'm furious I can't stop talking to you here, because all the words I've been saying would have no meaning, I can't stop because it would be like refusing to tell you how I got to this point, the whole conversation has been about communicating that to you, telling you how I got here, what called to me and when; and if I can't guess at what called me (in fact, I don't know), I can say how or when or at least what effect the call had on my soft flesh, how I felt my saliva dry up, my sweat cease to be, my blood turn to stone in my veins. If I'd stopped talking to you at the concert, I'd just be a nameless, overstrung girl; I'd just be my sea-blue corduroy little two-piece, my size three squeaky-clean leather shoes. If I were only that, I wouldn't be ashamed, why or of what? I wouldn't need to tell anyone; I wouldn't need the somber voice I've used, taken hold of, to reach out to you.

So I'll have to take my memories to their conclusion, to the point they reach, to the moment when the flow of what might feed them halted, when they were lopped and no bud remained.

Nobody was at home. That had never happened to me: nobody was there. My sisters had gone to visit their grandmother, something they now did frequently. In fact, they'd resurrected her since Esther's death, plucking her from nothingness with a vigorous, pleading affection that I interpreted as their greatest deceit. From never visiting her, they now had a program of almost daily visits, because if they had lost their Mom in circumstances nobody ever explained to me, they weren't prepared to be without a Mom again, and leapt into her frozen arms to protect themselves from death.

There was nowhere I could leap. Grandma couldn't bear the death of her child: along with her I had been erased from her gaze, had faded and lost the form her affection had granted me and that I so appreciated. When I looked her in the eyes the memory of Esther came between me and her—Esther's face when she was my age, when she was younger than me, when she was going to give birth to me, when she went to New York to receive her prize…Between Grandma and myself the reflection of Esther, a curtain of tears that prevented my approaching her without drowning in sorrow…

Everyone realized this. People knew I was her favorite, that I was the preferred granddaughter. Now people knew I was a piece of inert flesh who had to be cared for, whom people mentioned with worried looks: *Poor girl! Who will look after her?*

So my sisters were out. And Dad? He was out. Shut off by themselves in their room, inaccessible, the maids were out as well; they'd asked permission to go out. Where had Dad gone?

Why had they left me alone? I was afraid, this time afraid of everything and everybody. Not only what pursued me was a threat, what surrounded me was too: my white bedroom curtains, curtains alive like insects, like animals caged in a zoo I wouldn't want to visit, slumbering beasts awoken and enraged by my presence. And the curtains were nothing by the side of the stormy sea, the sea of the floor of the house! Who could step without risking their leather on the cruel wood, the greedy carpet, the silvery beams from a light that didn't reveal what surrounded me, but spotlighted me as the enemy to be attacked?

I began to feel the problem wasn't in the house and with me:

the threats from everything that wasn't persecuting me were merely an indication that something fatal was being plotted outside the house. I switched on the radio and sat down to listen, lying back in the armchair to hear what fatality had descended over the city. I listened to the announcer's warm voice introducing songs, listened to the songs, and felt my whole body on the sofa waiting for the fatal news to interrupt the flow of the radio: those who had left the house (I was convinced of that much) couldn't return, couldn't cross the flames or the dense layers of smoke or the flood or the explosion or whatever had happened out there. I stretched myself out alone in the armchair, in the house they'd all finally abandoned because they knew it was inhabited by the one who'd left them forever and that it was my fault.

When I woke up it was already night, early or deep into the night I wasn't sure. Nine, ten, twelve, three a.m.? Who knows what time it might be. Had somebody come home? I walked over to Dad's room: asleep, and even snoring. My sisters weren't in. Who knows if the maids had returned? Esther hadn't. I went to my room. Sat on the edge of my bed, unfastened my shoes, and was going back to sleep in yesterday's clothes, clothes which for the first time in my life hadn't been removed and changed for nightwear, and there, from my shod feet I saw them all looking up at me, my pursuers looking at me from my own feet as if from the window of a high building which they inhabited. I felt real panic! From my feet? And where were my shoes? I spotted the shoes I was wearing a moment before in their rightful place in the vertical shoe rack that hung at one end of the wardrobe.

I ran barefoot from my bedroom, not knowing where to look,

not wanting my gaze to linger on myself, I didn't want to see myself, didn't want to see who I was or what I was looking for or where I was going; fear struck me down: I had no strategy for trying to escape from my pursuers. I ran and ran and ran. Never walking. Never looking where I was heading. I had lost everything.

When I opened my eyes, I was opposite the door leading to the street. What was I intending to do? Leave the house? Go where?

Had the disaster outside happened? I thought I caught the smell of smoke, air thick with small, carbonized particles, still glowing, because they cruelly stuck to my body. My breathing burnt me. I tried to open the door to the street but couldn't—it was stronger than I was. My pursuers were there. I could hear them breathing next to me. I felt they would harass me no more and, instead of relief, my body ceased to weigh on the earth; my body was weightless: my body reached upward, obeyed a different pull of gravity. I fixed my gaze on an area of the garden, sought solace there. A hole, a hole as if dug out by an animal revealed a heart beating beneath the earth, a heart like a frog's but much bigger. I stooped down, picked up the heart in my right hand, held it, clenched my fist around it. My pursuers departed, my body regained its own weight, filled with weight at this contact with the warm heart the earth had given up to stop me: a warm, dry heart, soft but strong as if made of wood or leather. It palpitated. I held on tightly.

My panties were wet; the white cotton impregnated by liquid warm like the heart. They were soaked and I felt it so distinctly, a warm liquid beginning to trouble me, running down my thighs. What was it? What was running from inside me, betraying me?

Soon, from the moment I saw the house lights come on and heard Dad call me, I could see my white socks stained with the same blood I knew had stained my panties and legs. What had snapped inside me? I thought: "It's because I dreamed no more," because another night I thought the thread holding them, like the electricity cable in the eucalyptus, would at any time lash out inside me. "Is that right?"

Why did I think that? Because I'd let myself be defeated and, at a loss, was contemplating my own defeat too late. Then I thought: "Don't be foolish, it's the heart you're holding!" And I let go. Then my body, with no other defense, now weightless, couldn't stay a moment more and went up, up, and up, accompanied by those who had always pursued me.

I saw Dad come out and shout my name in the garden. I heard him run to the phone, I saw him (how did I see this?) find me in bed, in my pajamas, with my clothes scattered untidily over the floor... I was asleep, or rather, she, his daughter, was sleeping forever, in flannel pants soaked in blood, on stained sheets, her eyes closed, her face set in an undeservedly serene expression.

The doctor could not tell him why I had died.

CARMEN BOULLOSA is one of Mexico's leading novelists, poets, playwrights, and essayists. She has published eighteen novels, two of which were designated the Best Novel Published in Mexico by the prestigious magazine *Reforma*—her second novel, *Before*, also won the renowned Xavier Villarutia Prize for Best Mexican Novel. Her most recent novel, *Texas: The Great Theft* won the 2014 Typographical Era Translation Award, was shortlisted for the 2015 PEN Translation Award, and was nominated for the 2016 International Dublin Literary Award.

PETER BUSH is an award-winning literary translator of Spanish, Catalan, French, and Portuguese from Oxford, UK. Peter was Professor of Literary Translation at Middlesex University and later at the University of East Anglia where he also directed the British Centre for Literary Translation. Recent translations include Fernando Royuela's *A Bad End*, Emili Teixidor's *Black Bread*, and Jorge Carrion's *Bookshops*.

Thank you all for your support. We do this for you, and could not do it without you.

DEEP VELLUM

DEAR READERS,

Deep Vellum Publishing is a 501c3 nonprofit literary arts organization founded in 2013 with the threefold mission to publish international literature in English translation; to foster the art and craft of translation; and to build a more vibrant book culture in Dallas and beyond. We seek out literary works of lasting cultural value that both build bridges with foreign cultures and expand our understanding of what literature is and what meaningful impact literature can have in our lives.

Operating as a nonprofit means that we rely on the generosity of tax-deductible donations from individual donors, cultural organizations, government institutions, and foundations to provide a of our operational budget in addition to book sales. Deep Vellum offers multiple donor levels, including the LIGA DE ORO and the LIGA DEL SIGLO. The generosity of donors at every level allows us to pursue an ambitious growth strategy to connect readers with the best works of literature and increase our understanding of the world. Donors at various levels receive customized benefits for their donations, including books and Deep Vellum merchandise, invitations to special events, and named recognition in each book and on our website.

We also rely on subscriptions from readers like you to provide an invaluable ongoing investment in Deep Vellum that demonstrates a commitment to our editorial vision and mission. Subscribers are the bedrock of our support as we grow the readership for these amazing works of literature from every corner of the world. The more subscribers we have, the more we can demonstrate to potential donors and bookstores alike the diverse support we receive and how we use it to grow our mission in ever-new, ever-innovative ways.

From our offices and event space in the historic cultural district of Deep Ellum in central Dallas, we organize and host literary programming such as author readings, translator workshops, creative writing classes, spoken word performances, and interdisciplinary arts events for writers, translators, and artists from across the world. Our goal is to enrich and connect the world through the power of the written and spoken word, and we have been recognized for our efforts by being named one of the "Five Small Presses Changing the Face of the Industry" by Flavorwire and honored as Dallas's Best Publisher by *D Magazine*.

If you would like to get involved with Deep Vellum as a donor, subscriber, or volunteer, please contact us at deepvellum.org. We would love to hear from you.

Thank you all. Enjoy reading.

Will Evans
Founder & Publisher
Deep Vellum Publishing

LIGA DE ORO ($5,000+)

Anonymous (2)

LIGA DEL SIGLO ($1,000+)

Allred Capital Management
Ben & Sharon Fountain
Judy Pollock
Life in Deep Ellum
Loretta Siciliano
Lori Feathers
Mary Ann Thompson-Frenk
   & Joshua Frenk
Matthew Rittmayer
Meriwether Evans
Pixel and Texel
Nick Storch
Social Venture Partners Dallas
Stephen Bullock

DONORS

Adam Rekerdres
Alan Shockley
Amrit Dhir
Anonymous
Andrew Yorke
Anthony Messenger
Bob Appel
Bob & Katherine Penn
Brandon Childress
Brandon Kennedy
Caroline Casey
Charles Dee Mitchell
Charley Mitcherson
Cheryl Thompson
Christie Tull
Daniel J. Hale

Ed Nawotka
Rev. Elizabeth
   & Neil Moseley
Ester & Matt Harrison
Grace Kenney
Greg McConeghy
Jeff Waxman
JJ Italiano
Justin Childress
Kay Cattarulla
Kelly Falconer
Linda Nell Evans
Lissa Dunlay
Marian Schwartz
   & Reid Minot
Mark Haber

Mary Cline
Maynard Thomson
Michael Reklis
Mike Kaminsky
Mokhtar Ramadan
Nikki & Dennis Gibson
Olga Kislova
Patrick Kukucka
Richard Meyer
Steve Bullock
Suejean Kim
Susan Carp
Susan Ernst
Theater Jones
Tim Perttula
Tony Thomson

SUBSCRIBERS

Adrian Mitchell

Aimee Kramer

Alan Shockley

Albert Alexander

Amber Appel

Amrit Dhir

Andrea Passwater

Anonymous

Ashley Coursey Bull

Barbara Graettinger

Ben Fountain

Ben Nichols

Bill Fisher

Bob Appel

Brandye Brown

Carol Cheshire

Chase Marcella

Cheryl Thompson

Chris Sweet

Cody Ross

Cory Howard

Courtney Marie

Courtney Sheedy

David Christensen

David Weinberger

Ed Tallent

Erin Kubatzky

Frank Merlino

Greg McConeghy

Ines ter Horst

James Tierney

Jeanne Milazzo

Jennifer Marquart

Jeremy Hughes

Jill Kelly

Joe Milazzo

Joel Garza

John Winkelman

Jonathan Hope

Julia Rigsby

Julie Janicke

Julie Janicke Muhsmann

Justin Childress

Ken Bruce

Kenneth McClain

Kimberly Alexander

Lara Smith

Lea Courington

Lissa Dunlay

Lucy Moffatt

Lytton Smith

Marcia Lynx Qualey

Margaret Terwey

Mark Shockley

Martha Gifford

Martha Gurvich

Matt Bull

Meaghan Corwin

Michael Elliott

Michael Holtmann

Neal Chuang

Nhan Ho

Nick Oxford

Owen Rowe

Patrick Brown

Peter McCambridge

Robert Keefe

Sam Ankenbauer

Scot Roberts

Shelby Vincent

Steven Kornajcik

Steven Norton

Susan Ernst

Tim Connolly

Tim Kindseth

Todd Jailer

Todd Mostrog

Tom Bowden

Zachary Hayes

AVAILABLE NOW FROM DEEP VELLUM

MICHÈLE AUDIN · *One Hundred Twenty-One Days*
translated by Christiana Hills · FRANCE

CARMEN BOULLOSA · *Texas: The Great Theft* · *Before*
translated by Samantha Schnee · translated by Peter Bush · MEXICO

LEILA S. CHUDORI · *Home*
translated by John H. McGlynn · INDONESIA

ALISA GANIEVA · *The Mountain and the Wall*
translated by Carol Apollonio · RUSSIA

ANNE GARRÉTA · *Sphinx*
translated by Emma Ramadan · FRANCE

JÓN GNARR · *The Indian* · *The Pirate*
translated by Lytton Smith· ICELAND

NOEMI JAFFE · *What are the Blind Men Dreaming?*
translated by Julia Sanches & Ellen Elias-Bursac · BRAZIL

JUNG YOUNG MOON · *Vaseline Buddha*
translated by Yewon Jung · SOUTH KOREA

FOUAD LAROUI · *The Curious Case of Dassoukine's Trousers*
translated by Emma Ramadan · MOROCCO

LINA MERUANE · *Seeing Red*
translated by Megan McDowell · CHILE

FISTON MWANZA MUJILA · *Tram 83*
translated by Roland Glasser · DEMOCRATIC REPUBLIC OF CONGO

ILJA LEONARD PFEIJFFER · *La Superba*
translated by Michele Hutchison · NETHERLANDS

RICARDO PIGLIA · *Target in the Night*
translated by Sergio Waisman · ARGENTINA

SERGIO PITOL · *The Art of Flight* · *The Journey*
translated by George Henson · MEXICO

MIKHAIL SHISHKIN · *Calligraphy Lesson: The Collected Stories*
translated by Marian Schwartz, Leo Shtutin,
Mariya Bashkatova, Sylvia Maizell · RUSSIA

SERHIY ZHADAN · *Voroshilovgrad*
translated by Reilly Costigan-Humes & Isaac Stackhouse Wheeler · UKRAINE

COMING FALL/WINTER 2016–2017 FROM DEEP VELLUM

CARMEN BOULLOSA · *Heavens on Earth*
translated by Shelby Vincent · MEXICO

ANANDA DEVI · *Eve Out of Her Ruins*
translated by Jeffrey Zuckerman · MAURITIUS

JÓN GNARR · *The Outlaw*
translated by Lytton Smith· ICELAND

CLAUDIA SALAZAR JIMÉNEZ · *Blood of the Dawn*
translated by Elizabeth Bryer · PERÚ

JOSEFINE KLOUGART · *On Darkness*
translated by Martin Aitken · DENMARK

SERGIO PITOL · *The Magician of Vienna*
translated by George Henson · MEXICO

EDUARDO RABASA · *A Zero-Sum Game*
translated by Christina MacSweeney · MEXICO

BAE SUAH · *Recitation*
translated by Deborah Smith · SOUTH KOREA